D1187551

TEXAS FRIDAYS

SAN ANTONIO

SAM MOUSSAVI

San Antonio
Texas Fridays

Written by Sam Moussavi

Published by EPIC Press™
PO Box 398166
Minneapolis, MN 55439

Printed in the United States of America.

Cover design by Kali Yeado
Images for cover art obtained from iStockPhoto.com
Edited by Gil Conrad

LIBRARY OF CONGRESS CATALOGING-IN-PUBLICATION DATA

Names: Moussavi, Sam, author.
Title: San Antonio / by Sam Moussavi.
Description: Minneapolis, MN : EPIC Press, 2017. | Series: Texas Fridays
Summary: James Baker has earned one of the starting wide receiver positions at Churchill High School in San Antonio, Texas. During an early-season scrimmage, Baker takes a blow to the head and suffers a bad concussion. As a result, he must decide between his long-term health and a shot at making an impact on the field.
Identifiers: LCCN 2016946212 | ISBN 9781680764963 (lib. bdg.) | ISBN 9781680765526 (ebook)
Subjects: LCSH: High school—Fiction. | Football—Fiction. | Football players—Fiction. | Life change events—Fiction. | Young adult fiction.
Classification: DDC [Fic]—dc23
LC record available at http://lccn.loc.gov/2016946212

EPICPRESS.COM

For those eager to take liberties with the imagination and stay awhile.

—Pete Simonelli

1

James Baker's high school football career was difficult to label. As a freshman and sophomore, he played on the JV team, and played well enough, though nothing that brought on the attention of scouts, or even his own coaches. As a junior, Baker was one of the final players to make the team—not a good sign for a player who wanted to make an impact on Friday nights.

The summer between his junior and senior seasons was the turning point. Baker lived in the weight room of Churchill High School. When he wasn't lifting, he ran sprint after sprint on the field behind Churchill. While many of his more established teammates enjoyed their summer, Baker toiled under the Texas sun. He rebuilt his body and—for good measure—added speed.

His goal was to be one of Churchill's starting wide receivers before the first game of his senior season.

Churchill's wide receiver coach, Ernest Hayes, had made it all the way to the NFL, where he bounced around with three teams during a three-year career. Brief as his pro football career was, Hayes had still learned a thing or two about playing the wide-receiver position at the highest level. Baker realized during his transformative summer that he had a fantastic guide in Coach Hayes. They worked together extensively as Baker moved toward his goal of starting on opening night.

Hayes and Baker stood on the fifty-yard line of Churchill's practice field.

"I didn't realize you had these big hands," Hayes

said, before chuckling, "because you never had any reps. But you're here now."

"That's right," Baker replied.

As was Baker's new custom, he beat all of his other teammates out onto the field before Churchill's first practice of the season. He had to let them know—coaches, players, even the water boys—that his mission was for real.

"What's your responsibility on Z-short motion, X-over, nine-seventy-seven opposite?" Hayes asked out of the blue.

Baker looked up and scoffed a little under his breath, as if the question itself was an insult to his intelligence. "Motion down next to the tight end, wait for him to release, and then run my corner route seven yards deeper than the tight end runs his out-cut."

"Are you the primary receiver on this play?"

Baker shook his head vehemently. "No, my purpose is to influence the safety. Free the tight end up for an intermediate gain."

Hayes held his hand out for Baker to slap. Baker didn't smile while he did it though. This was the job that he had been preparing for all summer. He didn't need a pat on the back for knowing how to do his job.

Slowly but surely, the rest of Baker's teammates joined him and Hayes out in the San Antonio sun. There was Jake Ripley, Churchill's starting quarterback and a senior as well. Baker had also worked on his relationship with Ripley over the summer and felt that his QB had gained a healthy modicum of trust in him. The team's best player, Lucky Whitlock, sprinted out onto the field after Ripley. Whitlock played both ways—meaning he played both offense *and* defense—and could play nearly an entire game that way if the situation called for it. Whitlock's position of priority was running back. On defense, he doubled as one of the Chargers' best cornerbacks. Baker didn't have much of a relationship with the running back/defensive back because Whitlock didn't do much training over the summer, choosing instead to rest his body for the grind to come.

The last person to exit the locker room and walk onto the practice field was Churchill's head coach, Monty Forester. Forester was a true veteran of both the most recent Iraq War and Texas high school football. He was relatively young to be so experienced, but Churchill's athletic director thought that having a young coach was necessary, what with the new generation and all.

Baker liked Coach Forester because he was straight up with him. Forester played his best players based on the work they put in at practice and kept them in the game based on the notion of game day production. With these facts, there was no doubt in Baker's mind that once Forester witnessed his newfound commitment *and* chops, Baker would be in the starting lineup come opening night.

"Here's Coach," Hayes said. "This is your time."

"I'm ready," Baker said.

Coach Forester looked exactly like the Marine

he'd been in a former life. His body was fit and tight, his hair cropped within a sixteenth of an inch. He didn't allow any of Churchill's players to have differing or otherwise unruly hairstyles. No, Forester wanted uniformity. Baker didn't mind. With the summer heat in full effect, Baker opted to avoid the rigamarole of finding an acceptable hairdo and shaved his head bald.

Baker caught Ripley's attention with a chin nod, and Ripley, in turn, grabbed a ball to warm up. He zipped passes down to Baker, who was standing ten yards away. Forester stalked around the field pensively as his troops loosened up before the first practice of the new season. He focused on the new crop of underclassmen, eying them to ascertain who had worked over the summer, and who had slacked.

The season before had brought both joy and sorrow for the Chargers. Churchill went nine and one during its regular season, winning by an average of two touchdowns per contest. The sudden shock of defeat came during the first round of the Five-A Division-One Playoffs, where the Chargers were stunned by O'Connor High School by the score of twenty to seventeen. Ripley had thrown a late interception in the fourth quarter, and O'Connor turned the miscue into a last-second, game-winning field goal.

Now the Chargers had to overcome the graduation of ten seniors, a symmetrical five on offense, and five on defense, who had occupied starting spots the season before. Other than Ripley and Whitlock, Forester didn't know what he had in his team. And like war, Forester could not expect to know how a young football player would react until the bullets were live.

In true Marine form, practice started with a single whistle from Forester. No shouts, no bellows, no rah-rah attempts at manufactured emotion. No slogans. This was the time to work, not to talk about working.

Even Churchill's pre-practice stretching period

was calibrated to the precise specs of its coach. He wanted five lines of ten, give or take a few bodies, and he wanted seniors heading up the five lines. The team called out their stretches in military cadence which made the field sound both solemn and alive. Churchill's practices seemed austere because Forester didn't allow any joking around, though if it bothered the players, they rarely, if ever, showed it. Hard work without showmanship had been implanted into the program's DNA over the course of the coach's four seasons with the team.

The stretch came to an end, and it was finally time for Baker to show his stuff. After Forester broke the team into individual position groups, Baker followed the rest of the receivers to the far end of the field, where they would work with the quarterbacks.

Churchill's receiver group was one of the youngest and most inexperienced groups on the team. The starters from a season ago were graduated, and the team's third receiver was no longer at Churchill after transferring to another school in the off-season. This all meant that the team had not only to replace the production of three receivers, but also to reproduce the trust that Ripley had with his veteran-laden receiver group from the season before—a trust that could be hammered at during practice and forged during games.

Baker was first in line, taking the initiative to get down to the other end of the field before his teammates. Without an experienced receiver to bully his way to the front of the line, Baker had first dibs at building trust with Ripley.

Ripley bent down and took a simulated snap from the team's quarterback coach, then lofted a perfectly thrown go route to Baker thirty yards down the field. For all the hand wringing around San Antonio over Churchill's inexperience at the wide receiver position, the team's candidates all *looked* good. All of the receivers were tall, lean, and speedy. They each possessed an equal amount of chisel and tone. Baker was at the top of that list, coming in at six-foot-two, one hundred ninety pounds.

These warmup routes on air—without the hassle of defenders—were to be completed without incident, no questions asked. And they were. Not one ball hit the ground.

Forester nodded to Hayes, letting his receiver coach know that it was time to bring the gloves out. Hayes jogged over to the sidelines and produced a pair of boxing gloves from a long, neon orange equipment bag. Normally, such an action on a football field would bring about stares of inquisition, complete with head scratches, but not at Churchill.

Hayes fitted the gloves onto his large hands, trotted back onto the field, and took his place five yards in front of Baker. The gloves also served a symbolic purpose, a reminder that when a player is out on the football field, it's a fight.

Ripley took the next simulated snap. Baker shot

out of his stance toward Hayes, who swung at Baker to disrupt the receiver's timing as he weaved in and out of his brakes.

Baker took Hayes's two-piece combo at the top of his dig route, and Ripley delivered a perfect ball. Baker caught the pass in stride.

"Yeah," Hayes said, as Baker returned to the line of receivers, "take the contact and don't let it disrupt you."

Baker nodded and quietly ran back to the drill. Forester hadn't batted an eye because he was busy with the defense during that particular rep. Deep down, however, Baker knew he was a different player. It was only a matter of time before Forester took notice.

After ten more minutes of reps with the boxing gloves, it was time for Churchill's defensive backs to join the fray. In one of the truest expressions of Churchill's football mission, its defensive backs prided themselves on playing tight, physical, man-to-man coverage. The philosophy came from

Forester and his quest for all-out competition, *especially* when it was his players competing against one another. Forester was no fool, however; during real games against other schools, his defense employed the use of various zone coverages.

The first rep against a defensive back went to Baker, and he beat the press-man coverage with a nifty, out-in jab step. After losing the defender, Baker then turned on the jets and caught a seam route forty yards down the field. The play caused a few faint *ooh*s and *ahh*s on Churchill's otherwise church-quiet practice field.

Forester looked up from his vantage point at midfield. "Atta baby, Baker!" he called out, arms crossed over his barrel chest.

Baker ran back to the end of the receiver line. Instead of basking in the successful rep, he thought about how the cornerback might adjust on the next one.

In the spirit of competition, the cornerback from the opening rep enacted a measure of revenge on

Baker during the second rep. This time, he got a good jam at the line, disrupting Baker's timing on a slant route. The cornerback was able to knock down Ripley's pass, without ever giving Baker a realistic chance at the ball.

"Good play," Baker said to the DB.

The DB nodded and both players ran back to their proper places.

Baker put his hands on his hips and whispered, "Footwork. Jab step left and then go right."

The same player stepped in front of Baker for the rubber match. Baker accepted the cornerback's jam at the snap of the ball, and instead of using strength to overcome the coverage, he used the defender's forward momentum to slip by the press. With that nifty move, Baker ran his nine route down the sideline, leaving the cornerback in his wake.

He ducked his head like an Olympic sprinter and put a hand up in the air—*a la* Randy Moss—signifying he was open. Ripley saw the hand and released a bomb that traveled sixty yards in the air. The ball appeared to have been overthrown, but Baker busted it anyway. He started to make up ground, and just when it seemed like it was out of reach, he dove. He stretched out, and the ball dropped into his hands. He cradled it, as if it were a mottled, oblong baby. The catch evoked elation from Churchill's players and coaches, an uncommon occurrence for this early in the season.

Forester gave Baker a tap on the back of the helmet when the receiver got back to where the rest of the offense stood. Baker responded with a simple and humble nod to his coach.

We may have something here, Forester thought to himself as his team took a water break. *I like guys who dive.*

The end of the practice scrimmage was Baker's next opportunity to lay claim to a starting receiver spot.

With another sound of Forester's whistle, the scrimmage began. It pit the number one offense against the number one defense. For what it was worth, Baker was slotted as the starting flanker, or "Z"—the receiver that lines up on the same side of the field as the tight end. Forester believed that the position suited Baker because it called for a more physical type of receiver. Baker didn't care where he lined up; he just wanted to contribute. Ripley gave the offense the play call in the huddle: a toss-sweep to Lucky Whitlock. Baker processed the information and recalled his responsibility. The huddle parted with a collective "Break!" then Ripley settled underneath center.

Baker smiled right before the snap. A quiet confidence coursed through his body, stemming from an understanding of his responsibilities. He realized that he wasn't a player who was simply happy to be out on the field anymore. This actualization of potential was nice but short-lived, as the immediacy of the center snapping the ball impelled Baker to explode off the line.

The ball was pitched to Whitlock. Baker influenced the cornerback in front of him to take a false step inside, and just when he felt Whitlock coming up on his heels, he sealed the cornerback, putting his entire frame into the block. Whitlock hit the resulting hole in full stride and took the ball down the right sideline, untouched and into the end zone.

Baker ran back to the huddle amid the barks and helmet-slaps of his teammates. Hayes met him in front of the huddle and put his hand on the back of Baker's helmet.

"Smile," Hayes said.

"Not yet, Coach."

Baker entered the huddle and Ripley called out the second play. Forester liked to observe his team's scrimmages from behind the offense. The whistle was between his lips, and his arms, as always, were crossed. *Baker is making it so we* have *to acknowledge him. Let's give him a little more to do and see how he reacts*, Forester thought.

The whistle bleated from behind the huddle. Ripley stepped out of it and eyed Forester. The rest of the players in the huddle focused their attention inwardly.

"Come here, Jake," Forester said.

Ripley ran over.

"Let's change it up," Forester said.

"Okay."

"X-Zoom, seven-eighty-six. Tell Baker to let the tight end clear before he breaks off his dig."

"Got it," Ripley said.

"Oh and Jake," Forester said. "If Baker's even the slightest bit open, I want you to throw it to him."

Ripley nodded before running back into the huddle with the amended play call. Baker bit down on his mouthpiece and processed the information as Ripley broke the huddle.

The quarterback scanned the interior of the

defense as he waited to take the snap from center. Ripley then lifted his left leg and put the split end, or X receiver, on the opposite side of Baker, in short motion. The ball was snapped and Baker beat the press coverage at the line. The tight end ran his corner route right in front of Baker, just as Forester had called for. Ripley scanned the coverage and saw that Baker had also done the right thing, breaking his dig route into the middle of the field *after* the tight end cleared out first. Baker flashed open and Ripley threw a tight spiral, leading his receiver perfectly. Baker caught the ball in stride and out of harm's way. He cut up field and ran into the end zone. The play call itself was nothing special. A common dig route to the flanker is meant to gain twenty yards. Only when executed to perfection, with proper spacing and timing, does the route turn into a touchdown.

Baker didn't celebrate after his second big play of the scrimmage. He simply ran back to the huddle and flipped the ball to one of the water boys. The sun was at its peak. He took a bottle and squeezed a long stream of ice water down his back and then on his face.

2

BAKER FELT GOOD IN BOTH MIND AND BODY WHEN he got home after practice. He wasn't patting himself on the back though. Two plays stood out in his mind from the end of the scrimmage. On one running play he blocked the wrong man, and on the final play of the scrimmage, he ran a route at the wrong depth, causing an interception. Forester had chewed out Baker after both plays, but that part of it was not discouraging. Baker wanted his coaches on him. That meant he was making an impression.

His mother, Sandra, was not home when he walked into the kitchen looking for something to eat. She was not big on sports like most of the other mothers at Churchill High School. She wanted her son to focus on education first, as she had dedicated her life to academia. Sandra Baker was a full-time, tenure-track Humanities professor at the University of Texas–San Antonio campus, which was situated near the small, two-bedroom house they shared. Baker's father wasn't in the immediate picture, but the circumstance wasn't what most people assumed it to be when they heard that his father wasn't around. His father, Harold, was also a professor and taught out on the West Coast in California.

After the divorce, Harold's relationship with his son was mostly relegated to weekly phone calls and annual holiday trips. Harold, too, wanted Baker to take academics seriously, but was more supportive of his son's athletic pursuits than Sandra was. Baker missed his father, but had intuited enough to understand that maybe it was a good idea for his parents to be apart.

The front door opened and Baker turned as he crouched in front of the refrigerator.

"Hey," Sandra said, closing the door behind her.

"Hey, Mom," he said, focusing on the contents of the fridge again.

"I see you're scanning the contents of the fridge."

"Mmm hmm," he said.

She nodded as she approached the kitchen, lowering her light eyes to floor. Baker stepped aside and let her into the space in front of the fridge. While Baker had to make himself shorter to see inside, Sandra could simply bend to get a good look. Her petite frame mixed with her light skin gave her a child-like quality.

"Hmm," Sandra said, as she continued looking inside.

Sandra was a vegan. That meant she ate no products that came from animals. No eggs. No milk. No cheese. Not even honey. Sandra by no means forced Baker to live in the same radical way she did when it came to food, but she did try to steer him toward healthy eating in subtle and sometimes dishonest ways. Like the time she made Baker a "meat" lasagna with crumbled up tofu instead of ground beef. Baker didn't know the extent of his mother's subterfuge, gobbling up three platefuls, and for what it was worth, told Sandra that it was her "best lasagna ever."

"How was practice?" she asked.

"It went good, I think."

Baker wasn't one for words, but this didn't bother Sandra in the least. Her years spent as a "professional" student and then professor allowed her to realize that people can make contributions to society, no matter their individual disposition. His quiet nature meant that he was strong in some other facet of his personality, she thought.

"How was class?" he asked.

"It was really cool," she said. "I showed a 1954 documentary about World War II and then asked—forced, really—my students to run the discussion afterward. I wanted them to take *ownership* of it, you know? It evolved into this groovy, free-flowing type of thing."

"Nice," he said, then paused a moment. "Why are you teaching in the summer, anyway?"

When Baker and Harold weren't traveling in Europe together over his father's breaks from the classroom, Baker and Sandra traveled all over the United States and South America during her time off. This particular summer however, Baker had told Sandra that he wanted to stay in San Antonio to get ready for his senior season. Though he loved the ritualistic cycles of time alone with one parent in a strange and foreign place and the shared sadness at the ends of excursions of traveling with his parents, he felt the need to give football a real commitment in order to be successful.

"Well, since you didn't want to travel this summer," she said, "I decided to stay here and pick up a few extra classes. We could always use the money."

Baker nodded.

"And I also wanted to be near you," Sandra said, smiling.

Baker's brown cheeks shined red.

"You're gonna be going off to college soon. I have to get my time with you however I can."

"Hopefully it's on a football scholarship," he said.

"*However* it comes," she said sternly. "You're going away to college. Either way."

"If football doesn't work out, I don't understand why you think I shouldn't stay around here to go to college. There are plenty of good ones here in San Antonio."

"You should go to college somewhere else to expand your horizons. You won't realize your potential if you stay here."

Here came the "fullest and most realized potential" lecture.

"I remember when I left home at eighteen to go to NYU. All the way from Oakland," Sandra said. "The *East Coast*. Leaving home is in your blood."

"And if it's in my blood, why did Dad go back to California?"

"You have *my* blood racing through your veins, too," Sandra said. "Mine's better anyway."

She smiled.

"You don't think I can make it in football do you?" Baker asked. "That's where this is coming from."

"No, no, that's not true, James. I just think you need to be thinking realistically about your future. Football is fine. You can play for as long as you want. But you have to have a backup plan if it doesn't pan out. I mean, everybody wants a scholarship, but not everybody gets one. There are a lot of good players in Texas."

Baker nodded genuinely, and though he'd heard some version of this dialogue many times before, those talks were in the past. This new version of himself—with the grueling workouts transferring to production *on* the field—rendered Baker's athletic future a question mark. But not in a bad way. Before, there was slim to no chance that he'd play beyond high school. Now there were possibilities.

"And in *this* family, backup plan means college."

Baker sighed, "What are you making us for dinner?"

"Oh," she said. "I'm going to make the most delicious burger, but instead of meat, I'm going to use Portobello mushroom."

"Ugh."

"Go sit down and rest your dogs," Sandra said, nodding into the living room. "And I promise you, it'll be one of the most delicious things you've ever tasted."

"Okay."

Baker walked into the living room and studied the pictures on the wall, like he'd done numerous times. There was something about the pictures that gave him comfort. Sandra had a lot of her academic colleagues and prized students from over the years visit her and Baker in San Antonio. These were the people who populated the photos along the wall. Some of the people in the pictures brought back memories in Baker's mind. Others he couldn't remember. One constant in every one of the photos was that he and Sandra were smiling. Their relationship wasn't perfect by any stretch, but there was love and respect between them. Compared to many of his teammates' relationships with their single moms, the state of his and Sandra's was more than fine.

"Just put ketchup and mustard on it, like you would any old hamburger," Sandra said, handing a plate over to Baker that held a Portobello burger and some salad.

Baker took a bite and as usual, his mother was right.

"Mmm," he exhaled, "that's actually real good, Mom."

"See!"

Baker worked on the burger without another comment because it was that good.

"I was over in the science department this morning between classes, visiting with a colleague, and she told me about this study in the *New York Times* about head trauma in football. The concussion issue."

This was new territory for Baker. Sandra had never taken much of an interest in his athletic pursuits, and this was the first time she had ever mentioned an issue that specifically related to football. Usually, the dinner table discussions were led by Sandra and had to do with some documentary about tribal clashes in Africa or a play written by a feminist out of NYC. But on the concussion issue, well, Baker had thoughts and opinions.

"I know the article," he replied.

"Did you *read* the article?"

Sandra took a small bite of salad and eyed her son.

"Not the entire thing, but I got the gist. It seems like it's trying to get people to stop playing football."

"Don't get defensive, James."

"I'm not. I just think that these studies are done by a bunch of people who have never played football in their lives."

"That may or may not be true. But it's not the point. The point is that there are clear, physical dangers that come from playing football."

"Not for everyone," Baker shot back.

"It's just something to think about, that's all."

"I've been playing football for eight years, but I haven't had one concussion. And I've only had a couple of teammates that have had them before. Seriously, the girls' soccer team has had just as many. I didn't see *those* head injuries talked about in the article."

Sandra looked down at her plate.

"What? You don't want me to play?"

"It's your decision whether you play or not," she said. "The moment your head is at risk, that's where I come in."

Baker held his mother's stare with a calm exterior,

while a tremor inside him caused him to fidget with the silverware next to his plate.

3

BY THE END OF CHURCHILL'S FIRST WEEK OF PRACtice, Baker had secured the starting flanker spot with his attention-to-detail approach. A knack for making big plays in practice did not hurt his cause, either. His goal of a regular season starting spot was not locked inside an airtight case; nevertheless, the development was huge.

That Saturday, Churchill held its annual preseason intra-squad scrimmage under the lights. The stands were filled with students, parents, and boosters, though Baker's stomach was free of butterflies. As he stretched, his eyes scanned the horseshoe pattern that was Churchill's stadium. The visual of a venue filled to capacity was nothing new to him, and besides, he *welcomed* the responsibility of being relied upon by his coaches and teammates. It beat the alternative of getting to play when—and only when—the outcome of the game was long decided. Forester walked around the field and greeted every man on his team individually, as was his custom. When he reached Baker, his eyes gleamed and he extended a taut hand.

Baker shook Forester's hand firmly while looking him straight in the eye.

"Hey Coach."

"Keep doing what you're doing," Forester said. "You've opened a lot of eyes. And something tells me that the best is yet to come."

"Yes sir."

"I'm proud of the way you've worked."

"Thank you, Coach."

Forester moved on, and Baker allowed himself a sliver of a moment to enjoy his journey. He surgically extracted the joy out of his mind by focusing on his key during any given play. Once he was content with his preparation, he looked up into the stands again. The atmosphere was all you could ask for on a late summer night. The temperature was manageable—high eighties with a random breeze that made its way onto the field. From the sound of the crowd, the fans were as eager as the players to get the season started. Baker heard them bustling and congregating with the optimism that comes from a new start.

The rules of the intra-squad scrimmage were much like the rules of a regular season game with one glaring exception: under no circumstance was the quarterback to be touched. All of the other players on the field were fair game. Although Forester did not want his guys going low on one another or making any head-to-head shots, he did want his players to get used to being hit at full speed before the first game of the season.

Ripley, wearing the "don't lay a finger on me" red practice jersey, led the first string offense onto the field amid the chants of his surname by the capacity crowd. He leaned into the huddle and took a deep breath.

"Okay, boys!" he shouted over the din. "Let's go out there and give these folks something to really holler about!" He barked out the opening play call, an off-tackle run for Whitlock, and the huddle parted.

"Break!"

The play called for Baker to motion over to the weak side. Ripley set him in motion with an inflection in his cadence. "R-ed eighty-two! R-ed eighty-two!"

Baker motioned from right to left and set himself in between the X receiver and left tackle. The cornerback followed him across the formation, tipping off man-to-man coverage. Baker got set off the line of scrimmage to avoid an illegal formation penalty.

"Hut! Hut!"

The center snapped the ball, and Ripley turned and handed it to Whitlock going downhill. This long-developing run was a staple of any team that fancied itself a disciple of power football. The old school play could take the will of an opponent, if used effectively.

Baker released off the line of scrimmage and his mind went through the permutations of his responsibilities. If the cornerback in front of him jumped inside to try to make the tackle, Baker would have to cut him off. The cornerback did no such thing—flowing to the outside instead—so Baker forgot about him. The second option was to seek out the free safety and, at the very least, get in his way. He located the free safety, who was beelining for Whitlock in the hole. Baker ran over as fast as he could and threw a legal, crushing block on the safety. This sprung Whitlock, who accelerated off Baker's hip and got down the left sideline. Just like he had on the first day of practice, Whitlock scored solely because of Baker. Ripley helped Baker off the turf and put both hands on his helmet.

"Hell yeah!" Ripley yelled over a roar emanating from the stands.

If springing Whitlock wasn't enough for Baker,

being singled out by the PA announcer for his block was the *coup de grâce*. Baker refused to let any of it get to his head. He knew where he came from and how much effort the journey required. He was not about to boast, nor would he allow anybody to tell him how good he was just because of a few preseason blocks.

The water boys flanked both huddles as players from both sides took a breather. Baker took a couple of squirts from a bottle before passing it on.

After the hysteria of the long touchdown run drive subsided, Churchill's first string offense and defense got back to it. Ripley called the play in the huddle, and this time Baker was the primary option on a nine route. Ripley called out his cadence, and Baker lined up with a cornerback right over top of him, signifying man-to-man coverage.

"Hut!"

Ripley took the snap and dropped seven steps. Pressure from the blind-side defensive end forced him out of the pocket to his right. Baker beat the jam off the line of scrimmage and continued down the right sideline, a yard outside the hash mark. He flew with a sprinter's gait as the cornerback struggled to keep in step. The DB was not beaten to the point of submission though.

Both players competed all the way down the sideline. Ripley let the pass fly. Baker looked up, tracked the arc of the ball, and put his head down once again. He stuck out his arms, and the ball dropped right into his hands. He gripped it for dear life as the cornerback chopped down with his left arm. He'd kept possession all the way down to the turf on the sixty-six yard pass play. The conquered cornerback helped Baker off the turf. The two players exchanged pats on the back of the helmet, before trotting back to their respective huddles.

The fans marveled at the team's new and explosive weapon. No one in the stands knew who James Baker was, or whether or not this was more than preseason hype.

Back in the huddle, Ripley and Baker pounded fists.

"Nice effort on that one, Bake," Ripley said.

"Just throw it up there and I'm going to come down with it," Baker said.

Baker's outright confidence in his ascent wasn't shocking to Ripley. The QB had seen the effort that Baker had displayed in going for every catch in practice that week, and frankly, the signal-caller had seen enough to become a believer. There was simply no overlooking his new top receiver's competitive drive.

Though the comment counted as Baker's first public proclamation of what he planned to do on the field, and was a radical departure from his strict, nose-to-the-grindstone demeanor of the past, all of it—including the mild boast, soaring up the depth chart, and making uncanny plays—felt earned and natural. Perhaps this was where he belonged.

After the buzz of the big play dissipated, however, Baker realized some discomfort in the top of his right shoulder. It burned in that nagging, persistent sort of way. After hauling in the catch, he must've landed directly on the joint, jamming it into its socket. Baker was not coming out of the scrimmage though. There was no way he was going to let this slip through his grasp.

The next play call was a slant to Baker. Coach Forester called in the play personally because he wanted to see what kind of effort Baker could exhibit on back-to-back plays. Baker lined up to the right of the formation as he waited for the snap of the ball. This time, the defense showed zone coverage: corners off, safeties deep, linebackers light on their feet in preparation for coverage drops.

He knew he had to get across the face of the cornerback to ensure that Ripley had a window to throw the slant into. Crossing the face would also help Baker avoid a big hit from the charging middle linebacker. After the ball was snapped, Baker sprinted at a forty-five degree angle, right into the teeth of the defense. He crossed the face of the cornerback and showed Ripley his eyes. Ripley glanced at the heady middle linebacker, who had sniffed out the slant. The pass was a low one; only Baker could catch it, and if he did, there'd be enough time to avoid a head-on collision. Baker didn't look up to locate the linebacker. Instead, he leaned on the "spidey-sense"—that ability to *feel* the bodies around him—that all good football players possessed.

Plus, there was no use looking danger in the eye. It was always there. Every player who suited up knew there was always the chance of taking a clean shot, of getting popped, of "getting your bell rung." At this moment, though, it boiled down to simpler terms for Baker. Coach Hayes's ubiquitous words rang in his ears: "you know you're gonna get hit anyway, so you might as well catch it."

Baker lurched down and snagged the low ball amid oncoming traffic. He cradled it into his right arm as he narrowly avoided the heat-seeking middle linebacker. Baker weaved through the sea of bodies and beat the strong safety on a dead sprint into the end zone. Forester allowed himself a smile.

The sidelines and stands went bananas. What figured to be a rebuilding season, now had the feel of something much bigger—a deep and transformative ride. Forester had a track record of bringing a group of young men together to achieve something over their individual capabilities. This team could be like the others and maybe even better. With Ripley, Whitlock, and now James Baker, all outcomes were in play.

Baker didn't worry about the danger that almost came his way on the slant. He simply moved on to the next play. He was welcomed to the sideline by his coaches—first Hayes, then Forester. Next he was mobbed by teammates. For a player who didn't say much, being the center of attention had a strange sensation attached to it. That strangeness was also tinged with euphoria, and Baker certainly allowed himself to indulge in it all.

Baker had long since crossed the threshold of

having to prove things to himself, having cleared it during his grueling summer. Now he sat at the precipice where everything he did was a point made to those around him: his teammates, coaches, and opponents. He was ready for this. The moment was not too big for him.

The second-string offense and defense were on the field, as the first stringers took a series off. Baker's legs had tightened up, and by the time the starters had to go back out, there was sincere grab in his right hamstring. In past seasons, staying loose didn't apply to him because he was only getting a handful of snaps. As a key player, he would have to learn how to get his muscles loose, in between series, after halftimes, and quick changes after turnovers, and be ready to compete.

"You good, Bake?" Ripley asked in the huddle.

Baker finished with an impromptu stretch before meeting his QB's eye. "Yeah. Just needed a minute to stretch.

"You gotta stretch, superstar," Ripley said with a smile.

Baker didn't smile back. The nagging in his right hamstring had his attention at the moment. It wasn't severe, but substantial enough to give some consideration. Baker grabbed at the hamstring as he ran to his spot for the first play of the series. The play was a run to the opposite side of where Baker was. When the ball was snapped, Baker went hard, cutting off the corner on the backside, but his burst wasn't the same.

"You a'ight, dog?" the cornerback asked.

"Yeah," Baker said, through a wince.

Baker ran back to the huddle with his head down, clawing at his hamstring. He quickly pulled his hand back when he reached the huddle. He didn't want to acknowledge the discomfort in any way because he didn't want his teammates and coaches doing the same. If he didn't believe the pain was there, then maybe it wouldn't exist. Besides, he knew pain from his summer workouts. Pain was a temporary condition, an illusion.

Ripley gave the huddle the next play call and looked to Baker as if to ask, "You, okay?" Baker nodded back and ran to his spot, this time to the left of the formation. Ripley put Baker in motion from left to right. He got set before the snap, and when Ripley dropped back to pass, Baker was into his route. The play called for him to run a deep dig, the same route that he had exploded for a touchdown on during the first practice. The coverage was zone, meaning that Baker would have to be precise in his depth and timing. His vision would be crucial as well on this one—he couldn't simply rely on feel. To make this route work, Baker had to see where the defenders were situated. That information would inform how he'd run his route. The goal was to find a window in the zone, so that Ripley could deliver a safe pass, in rhythm.

Whereas straight-line running caused no issue, the tight hamstring affected his ability to make sharp cuts. As a result, Baker's in-cut was loose and imprecise. Thus, Ripley delivered the pass into a crowd. To Baker's credit, he caught the ball for a twenty-yard gain. Problem was, he took a helmet-to-helmet hit from the free safety patrolling the deep half of the field.

The thunderclap from the direct hit caused a collective shudder from everyone in the stadium. Baker lay still on the turf, his right arm clutching the ball. He opened his eyes and looked up into what he thought was the sky. His vision refocused, and his hearing came back after a brief stint on mute. The sky was black, and Baker perceived the echoes of light around the fringes of his face-mask. *The overhead, stadium lights*, he thought. Then a rush of teammates, coaches, and trainers was on him, all of them looking down with a mix of inquiry and fear—that specific, helpless look of semi-horror that only those close to game hold on their faces after a collision of that magnitude.

"I'm okay," Baker said.

Baker wasn't sure if he was talking to one of his teammates, Forester, or simply blurting it out to make sure he still had the ability to speak. The team's head trainer, Nathan Miles, was crouched down next to Baker now.

"Where does it hurt, James?" Nathan asked. "Tell me where it hurts."

Baker moved his eyes from side to side and noticed that there was another pile-up like the one he was in the middle of right next to him. The free safety that hit him, he thought.

"I'm fine," Baker said to Nathan, fastening his eyes to the trainer. "I remember the hit and everything. How is Benny?"

Benny Tulane was the name of the free safety that put the hit on Baker.

Nathan looked over to where Benny was and then back to Baker. "Benny's doing okay," Nathan said. "We're checking him just like we're doing with you."

"I can get up."

"Okay," Nathan said before nodding at something in Baker's periphery.

Two of his teammates lifted him off the turf, and Baker steadied his body. He shook his head and there was a slight ringing in his ears. This was the hardest Baker had ever been hit on the football field.

"Hey," a voice said from behind.

There was a tap on Baker's shoulder.

Baker turned around and saw Kent Mortenson, a junior and second-string wideout.

"I got you," Kent said.

Baker nodded and walked off the field with the assistance of Nathan, guiding him as if he were blind. When he reached the sidelines, the crowd cheered him on.

"You okay?" Hayes asked, the first to meet Baker in front of the white line separating safety from danger.

"Just got my bell rung a little bit," Baker replied.

Forester hung over Hayes's shoulder. Baker met his head coach's eyes.

"That was a good shot," Forester said. "You didn't see him coming, huh?"

"Yeah, it was," Baker said, feeling angry and a little foolish. He realized now that the hamstring pull had contributed to the funky timing of the play. "I didn't see him."

"I want you to go over with Nathan. You're done for the scrimmage."

"Coach, I'm fine. Really." Baker's eyes widened. He felt them do so, and he hoped that the sheer size and the alertness within them would sway his coach.

Forester had seen worse hits in his football life, but also, recognizing the current, safety-first climate that football was trying to navigate and maybe even, survive within, didn't want to risk it with Baker. He would never say it out loud, but he appreciated Baker's toughness and willingness to go back out there. "We're just gonna check you out to make sure," Forester said. "You've done enough today anyway."

As Forester walked down the sideline and away

from him, Baker's shoulders slumped. Nathan was next in line to talk with Baker again, who at this point was a little tired of the conveyor belt after the big hit. Baker didn't understand what all the fuss was about. He was fine now. His body was simply not used to hits of that nature. Forester preached toughness, commitment, and responsibility. *How can I be any of those things if I'm on the sideline?* Baker thought.

"Hey James," Nathan said, putting his hand on Baker's back. "We're gonna go sit on the bench, and I'm gonna ask you a few questions. We'll go from there."

Baker looked out onto the field where his teammates were scrimmaging. He looked back to Nathan.

"Okay."

"Let me see your helmet," Nathan said with a smile.

Baker unbuckled his chinstrap and handed over his helmet. He followed Nathan to the bench. The crowd roared at a big play happening behind Baker.

How quickly they forgot his contributions to the team. He wanted to get back out there even more.

Baker sat down on the bench, and Nathan knelt down in front of him.

"What's your name?"

"James Baker."

"Where do you go to school?"

"Churchill High School."

"What city?"

"San Antonio."

"What state?"

"Texas."

"Where do you live?"

"1450 Vine Street."

"What's your mama's name?"

"Sandra."

"Daddy's?"

"Harold."

"What position do you play?"

"Wide receiver."

Nathan nodded.

"See?" Baker asked.

"Follow my finger," Nathan said, holding his right pointer finger in front of Baker's eyes. He did this so that he could track Baker's reaction time. If there was a concussion—minor or major—this test would reveal the onset of symptoms.

Baker saw Nathan's finger clearly and tracked it without incident. Nathan patted him on his knee. Baker heard the crowd as it oohed again.

"Just relax," Nathan said. "Breathe."

Baker took a deep breath that he felt all the way down to the balls of his feet. The pressure in his skull after the hit was exorcised with the breath. He looked into Nathan's eyes.

"I'm fine."

"You don't have a concussion," Nathan said. "This time. But there's something I'd like to talk to you about."

Baker's eyebrows raised involuntarily.

"Not now," Nathan said with a serious tone.

"We'll talk after the scrimmage. After you get showered and cooled off, come see me in my office."

Baker nodded.

"I'm gonna be closer to the field for the rest of the scrimmage," Nathan said, standing up. "You stay on the bench. Let me know if something is off, hear?"

"Okay."

Nathan walked over to Forester and said something into his ear. Baker knew what it was. He watched the rest of the scrimmage and among the many implications, the thing that resonated was Nathan's mandate to stay on the bench—a place Baker hated, a place where he promised himself he'd never be again. It was as if all the good things he'd done in the scrimmage and in practice up to that point had never happened.

4

FORESTER PRAISED THE TEAM IN THE LOCKER ROOM after the scrimmage. As was his preference, he did not single out players for their individual contributions, but rather framed both the good and the bad in a team context. He also didn't address Baker privately about the near concussion because it was his policy to leave medical situations up to the medical people.

The walk down to Nathan's office was a long one for Baker. He knocked twice on the closed door before Nathan called him in. The office was not an office at all; it was a room with two massage-style tables set up for the players to get their ankles taped. There was also an assortment of medical supplies and devices set in their proper places.

Nathan was busy kneading Whitlock's ankle when Baker walked in. Whitlock nodded and Baker reciprocated.

"I want you stay off it on your day off tomorrow," Nathan said. "I may even hold you out of practice early next week if the swelling doesn't go down by Monday."

"Aw, I'm good," Whitlock said. "You always trippin', Nathan."

"I'm serious. Don't be out running the town at all hours of the night. Don't be a social lion, hear? Your dream is to go pro, right?"

Whitlock's eyes lit up.

"Well, invest in your body, then," Nathan said. "Care for it."

Whitlock shook Nathan's hand and stood up to leave. He walked past Baker without a noticeable limp and that made Baker wonder. *Didn't Nathan just say that Whitlock is injured?* Baker thought.

Nathan opened his arms. "Welcome to my office, James," he said with humility.

"What's up, Nathan?"

"Sit," Nathan said, signing his name to a form that was locked into a clipboard.

Baker took a seat on one of the massage tables and waited for Nathan to finish.

Nathan dotted the page with his pen.

"How are you?"

"Fine," Baker said. "No headaches. No nausea. No blurred vision. I'm not sure why you wanted to see me."

"That's good—that you're not experiencing any symptoms."

Baker waited for the next series of questions or perhaps another battery of tests. When neither came, he sighed.

"What?" Nathan asked.

"I'm wondering what I'm doing here."

"Well, James, I just want to share my concern about what I saw with you out on the field tonight."

"I didn't have a concussion," Baker said, defensively. "You said so yourself. It was a just a tough hit. I just got my bell rung. That's all."

"See, *this* is what I'm concerned about."

Baker didn't understand; his eyes narrowed.

"This idea that you just had your bell rung, and that it wasn't a big deal. That hit was a big deal. All of them are. You can take a hit today," Nathan said with his pointer finger aimed at the floor. "One hit. And it could have long-term effects on your health. Memory loss. Depression. Even death."

Baker's eyes dilated and then focused.

"What I can't have is you not being honest with me," Nathan continued. "When you get injured out there, you need to tell me where the pain is and what symptoms you're experiencing. I called you in here because you seem to be a player who will go over the middle, draw attention, and get hit often. So I want to make sure we're cool and that you trust me. I'm here to help keep you safe."

Baker understood now.

"And that goes for the future *and* right now with this hit you took tonight. I'm going to be checking in with you the rest of the weekend to see if any symptoms creep up. You never know with head injuries."

"Did Coach Forester say anything to you about me?"

Nathan smiled. "Coach Forester knows everything that goes on with the team. He and I talk about all injured players. And he and I are on the same page. You are not to be hiding injuries to get back out on the field. Doing that doesn't help you or the team."

Baker nodded.

"We clear?"

"Clear," Baker said.

"Okay, make sure you track how you're feeling, especially when you get in bed. If you have any of the symptoms we talked about before—headaches, dizziness, light sensitivity—you call me on my cell phone. My number is on the sheet that I passed out before the first practice."

"Got it."

"Okay, go home and get some rest."

"Thanks. Oh, Nathan?"

"Yes?"

"How is Benny? I didn't see him in the locker room," Baker said.

"Benny did have a concussion. He's over at Methodist for evaluation."

Baker nodded before leaving Nathan's office and went back into the empty locker room. He sat down in front of his locker and let the conversation soak in. Baker knew Nathan meant well. As the head trainer, it was his responsibility to ensure player safety. Nathan's comment about Coach Forester was a bit surprising though. Forester was a Marine and by all accounts, including Baker's own from junior year, he was a tough, no-nonsense guy. Before the talk with Nathan, Baker assumed that Coach wanted his players to play through their injuries as much as humanly possible. But maybe Baker was wrong? Maybe his mother was onto something with her academic view of concussions?

His mind swam with all of these questions and then sunk when no clear answers presented themselves. What Baker knew was that there was no pain from the big hit, just noise caused by its aftermath. The other thing he knew was that he wanted to be out on the field. The responsibility of being relied upon, respected by teammates for his work on the field, left Baker wanting more.

5

"HOW DID THE SCRIMMAGE GO?" SANDRA ASKED with a knowing smirk. She was plating up some vegan enchiladas that smelled amazing—an awful lot like the real thing. Sandra couldn't make it to the scrimmage because she taught a summer workshop on modern feminism that met on Saturday afternoons. Baker didn't mind because all of Churchill's regular season games were on Friday nights. Sandra could and would make it to all of those affairs.

"It went fine."

"Nothing you wanna tell me?"

"Uh-uh."

"Nathan, the team trainer called me."

Baker looked up to the ceiling in disbelief. He was really starting to dislike Nathan. "What'd he say?"

"That you took a pretty big hit out there tonight."

Baker jabbed his fork into the food. "I'm fine, Mom. I just got my bell rung."

Sandra snapped her fingers theatrically. "Nathan told me you might say that."

"I'm *okay.* Look." He opened his eyes wide and looked into his mother's eyes.

"I'm supposed to monitor you tonight to see if you show any symptoms."

"I know all that."

"It's ironic that we talked about this very thing the other night," Sandra said. "I know you're almost a man, James. *Almost.* And a lot of what that article talked about is that these players who suffer concussions try to hide them because either they want to be seen as tough *or* they don't want to lose their spot on the team."

Sandra paused and sighed as she looked at her

son. “The worst part of the article was that the coaches and medical staff sometimes pressure players into playing through their injuries. Are your coaches pressuring you?”

“No. That stuff doesn’t happen at Churchill. It’s actually the opposite. I was fine and felt no symptoms, but they made it seem like my head was gonna fall off,” Baker said. “Nathan made it really clear to me after the scrimmage that he and Coach Forester are on the same page. If we’re hurt, we have to speak up.”

“That’s good. I’m thankful for that.”

“But I didn’t get a concussion. I went through all this testing with Nathan, and I’m fine.”

“This time. And I know you went through it with Nathan, but you didn’t go through it with me, so listen up.”

Baker sighed and sat back in his chair. He picked at his food.

“Look, I know this is a really big year for you, and you worked your butt off to become a contributing member of the team. This thing with the injuries, though. I can watch over you here at home all I want. That is, when I am here. Nathan can assess your symptoms and share his medical opinion with you every time he sees you at school. But it's up to you, James. At the end of it, you are the one who's going to have to make these decisions."

He watched his mother as she spoke, just as he always did. He loved his mother for many reasons, but two of them stuck out in his mind as they sat there together. She was persuasive and engaging when she spoke. He didn't know too many other guys on the team who had mothers that could speak like his did. Second, she treated him like a man. Even when he was little, she never babied him. She loved him, but not in a smothering way. He also knew that she was right—that when it came to injuries it would be up to him. He was the one out there on the field. No one forced him to play. That's why Nathan sat him down after the scrimmage in the first place.

"You'll have to ask yourself if it's worth it," she said.

"Huh?" Baker replied dreamily.

"James?" Sandra asked. "Do you hear me?"

He locked back in. "Yeah. I hear you, Mom."

"Good," Sandra said. "Now give me your thoughts on the vegan enchiladas."

With still no symptoms of a concussion, Baker took it easy and hung out with his mother some more before going to bed. With all the stuff about his head injury, he had forgotten all about his tight hamstring. He iced it periodically throughout the evening, before going upstairs to his room and into bed. Football had never been so complicated for Baker. It seemed a little silly that the adults around him were making it a life and death thing. As he lay in bed, he thought about specific plays, where the defenders were rallying from, and how he could avoid big hits in the future. He could also talk to Ripley, and they could work together to find windows for safe passage on the field. Baker had gained a real level of respect in the locker room with his play. He was sure that going to the starting quarterback with suggestions wouldn't be looked upon as blasphemous anymore.

It dawned on him that these thoughts had never occurred to him before in his football life—the idea that the life of a spot player is much different than that of a frontline player. He understood that every regular—those who played a bunch of snaps—was simply looking out for his long-term health. Yet he knew that with more time on the field, he'd learn how best to protect himself. These were among Baker's final thoughts before dozing off.

When he opened his eyes the next morning, a throbbing headache awaited him. With the pain came a pressure so severe and persistent that he could not move, let alone stand. He shifted his weight in bed and felt the sheets sticking to his body; he had sweated the entire night and had not even noticed. The only window in his room, the one above the far wall, was open, and there were a few morning rays streaking through. Each time Baker moved, his body gave a response that something was off. But none was worse than when his eyes coincided with the streaks of morning sunlight. To say his eyes were light sensitive would've been laughable because there was nothing sensitive about them. The light burned his eyes, and the more he fought it, the more it pained him. The stinging right behind his eyes nearly caused him to scream out. But a moment of instantaneous clarity—the thought of alerting his mother, and therefore the end of his playing days—put a fortuitous lump in his throat. Baker flung his head away from the window as if he wanted to separate it from his neck. He clutched the sheets and tried to stand. A wave of dizziness hit then. If he had not plopped right back down on the bed, he would have vomited. His chest heaved in a heavy, undulating rhythm now.

There was nothing for Baker to do but accept the pain, and *hope* that it was temporary. *If it's not hard to do, then what's the point?* he thought, and in another inexplicable moment of clarity, his mind flashed back to Lucky Whitlock in the trainer's room after scrimmage. Nathan's words of warning to Whitlock were just that. And like Whitlock, it was up to Baker now to either heed the warning or ignore it. Or perhaps there was a third way. Baker remembered Whitlock leaving the trainer's room without a limp.

Yes.

He could control his destiny if he wanted to. He would just have to be smarter, learn how to hide the pain. Baker closed his eyes tightly against the light, pain, and heavy indecisiveness.

* * *

About three hours later, it was as if none of it had

ever happened. The midday Texas sun was in full effect when Baker tentatively opened and shut his eyes a few times before opening them for good. He touched his temples without feeling any pain. He sat up slowly without any nausea. He looked over at the clock radio on his desk and saw it was eleven a.m. He stood up slowly without feeling dizzy. For good measure, Baker walked over to the window and popped his head out into the sun. His eyes could handle the light. If what he'd experienced earlier was just a warning, what would the real thing feel like?

Baker walked out of his room and down the hall toward the single bathroom he and his mother shared. He could hear Sandra downstairs listening to an old funk record—something from the seventies—and likely cooking a vegan lunch. In the bathroom, he stared at himself in the mirror over the sink for a while. He thought that the most logical place to start would be the eyes. Baker examined his eyes closely, looking for any kind of sign that predicted trouble. His vision was sharp; there was no blurred image staring back at him in the mirror. He looked like himself.

Then he began the same test that Nathan had put him through on the bench after the hit. He lifted his right pointer finger into the air and held it in front of his eyes. He moved the finger from left to right, right to left, tracking the movement several times. He watched his eyes in the mirror, as they followed the finger and from this too, everything seemed normal. His reaction time, focus, and attention span were as they normally were.

"What next?" he asked himself out loud. Memory. Baker remembered everything. The block he made on the first play of the scrimmage. The touchdown he scored. The hit. He could replay the hit in his mind, rewinding and fast-forwarding the action on command. The only thing he couldn't do in his mind was avoid the hit, because that would be make-believe.

"I'm fine," Baker said aloud, backing away from the mirror.

He took off his clothes and moved into the shower. The cold water fell down his back as he scrubbed the film of dried sweat off his chest, arms, and legs. *There's nothing to be afraid of until there is*, Baker thought, as he stepped out of the shower. He exited the bathroom to his mother's calls from downstairs.

"James?" she shouted. "You awake?"

"Yeah, Mom!" he called back.

"Good!" she said. "Come down and eat something."

"Be right down!"

Baker and his mother didn't spend a lot of time together outside of the house. They were both busy and often too tired to do anything beyond sit at the kitchen table and share a meal. He became excited as he changed for their day out together—excited and a little nervous. He didn't want his mother interrogating him all day with her eyes. Though their time together was sporadic, Sandra knew him well. If any trace of the way he'd felt the night before returned, his mother would realize it, and it would all be over.

“You *were* tired?” Sandra asked, as she and Baker sat in her Prius—she behind the wheel, Baker in the passenger seat.

“I guess I’m not used to playing this much,” Baker said with a smile.

“You’ve always been a hard worker. I’m glad you’re experiencing some positive results. It’s nice to see things pay off.”

“Where we going?” Baker asked.

Sandra smiled, staring straight ahead as she continued driving.

“Tell me where we’re going, Mom.”

Still no response from Sandra.

“I should’ve asked where we were going before I agreed to come.”

“What am I always telling you?” she asked. “Get *all* the information.”

“Seriously, where are we going?”

"First we're gonna stop by campus. There's a whole lot of stuff happening today," Sandra said "We can walk around, soak it all in, maybe grab a smoothie. After that, we can do whatever you want to do."

Baker nodded. He didn't mind going to UTSA's campus. He'd been there with her plenty of times. Early in high school, Baker used to meet Sandra on campus after football practice, on the days she taught evening classes.

"How do you feel?" Sandra asked, as they waited for a light to turn green.

"I'm fine," Baker said. "No symptoms. I feel like me."

"Good. You look like you."

The lying didn't sit well with him. Baker was not the type to lie. He wasn't even good at it. His mother always sniffed out his lies before they fully developed. When they'd first gotten into the car, he had been surprised she hadn't pressed him further. He'd decided that he must've been fine because his mother thought he looked fine. At any rate, he was symptom-free. The pain from the morning must have been imaginary: a bad dream.

"So?" Sandra asked.

"Yeah?"

"Any girls you like at school right now?"

"Mom."

"I'm just asking a question. Are you seeing any girls that you aren't introducing to your mother?"

"First of all, I'm not discussing this with you," he said. "And second, when would I have time for a girl right now?"

"That's true. But you should be spending at least some of your time with members of the opposite sex."

Baker eyed his mom with a quizzical fury.

"When I was in high school, I hung out with a lot of different boys—"

"Mom! I don't wanna hear about you being with a lot of dudes!"

"Not sexually, James! Get your mind out of the gutter."

Baker shook his head and put his forehead into his right hand.

"Are you having sex?"

"This conversation is over," Baker said. "For real."

"What?"

Mother and son laughed at the lack of boundaries that could only be explained by how close they really were. Sandra was all Baker had and vice versa. They both knew this, and it painted everyday of their life together.

His mother switched subjects. "Are you sure you want to spend all your time playing football?"

"As long as I can," Baker said.

"There are a lot of other things out there in the world, James."

"Not the college thing again."

"I'm not just talking about college," she said. "Painting. Movies. Hiking. Cooking. All I'm saying is that you have to see past this one thing. Life can't be just about football."

Baker kept quiet, opting to simply watch his mother as she drove.

"You are going to college though," Sandra added.

"You know what it is?" Baker said. "It's not just football. I mean, don't get me wrong. I love the game. But what really gets me going is the challenge. I mean, I came from nowhere. Literally. We moved around all the time, and I was never comfortable in school. And I'm quiet to begin with."

Sandra laughed.

"Seriously, though, now that I'm a starter, I'm a part of it. Whatever that thing is that makes a person feel needed and wanted, I finally found it. Football is that thing for me."

Now it was Sandra Baker's turn to watch her son as he spoke. She was proud of his drive, but even prouder of his mind, of the mentality that he had—the kind where a person wants nothing if it's not earned. Sandra used to worry about what kind of son she had when James was a child. She wanted a son who wouldn't be afraid of challenges. But as a woman, she didn't quite know how to instill such a quality in a young man. She wasn't even sure if it was possible to do so. Sandra had that brand of undeniable resolve in her personality. James's father, Harold, had it. And sure enough, James had it too.

6

Baker's head felt fine as he and Sandra walked around the student center at UTSA. Though no classes met on Sundays, the campus was alive with rallies, social events of questionable taste, and concerts put on by different student groups on campus. Sandra licked at a scoop of vegan vanilla ice cream sitting on top of a cone.

"Sure you don't want some ice cream?"

"That's not ice cream," Baker said.

"It's delicious! Here, try some."

Baker tasted the ice cream and she was right. "Damn! That does taste good!"

"Told you."

"But it's not ice cream," Baker said with a smile. "What are we doing here?"

Sandra spread her arms apart. "Just want you to see what a college campus feels like."

"I've been here before," he said. "Plus, all of the other campuses you've worked at."

"But this is different, James. You're grown now. And so close to attending college yourself."

Baker crossed his arms.

"By the way, have you thought of some schools that you want to apply to?"

"Can I just get through the football season first?"

"Okay, okay."

They continued walking around the student center, stopping to chat with colleagues and students of Sandra's. Baker thought it was cool. He didn't think the people at college were weird like some of his teammates at Churchill did. He secretly liked school and was actually excited about the idea of being a college student. Unlike most of his teammates, he knew all about the college environment through having two college professors as parents.

There was another important aspect about college that Baker learned about at a young age: women. He'd learned that girls became women in college and that the women in college couldn't be more different than the girls in high school. This idea sat at the forefront of Baker's mind as his mother talked with another professor from her department. He stood dazed, looking at all the beautiful women walking by. The temperature was pleasing, a rare break from the brutality of late summer in Texas. Fat, pillowy clouds muffled the full force of the sun and allowed an unobstructed view of the young women on campus. Some wore only bikini tops with cut-off shorts. Others wore low-cut summer dresses that flared off at the bottom. Baker saw many sets of long legs tanning in front of the student center. Sandra caught her son's gaze and smirked, even as her colleague went on about budget cuts and shady administrators. She nudged Baker with her elbow to go out front and mingle with the ladies.

Baker was emboldened by his mother's tacit dare. He ventured out into the main courtyard in front of the student center, where he found even more women than he'd expected, throwing Frisbees or simply relaxing with friends. Women of all colors and shapes were represented. Though quiet, Baker was not shy when it came to the opposite sex. But he was not one of those clowns who walked up to a woman, spouting off inane compliments. He'd had one serious girlfriend during high school—serious because they'd had regular sex and even talked about going to college at the same place. The relationship went by the wayside because of football, though neither Baker nor the girlfriend ever fully realized what went wrong.

This past summer he made a decision—no serious relationships until college. Just football. In retrospect, his single-mindedness about making an impact on Churchill's football team during his senior season was likely what drove his girlfriend away for good. He was now free to do what he pleased. And when he walked through the throng of women, he could see just what his mother was talking about when she preached the benefits of college. This was pretty sweet. Everyone looked so carefree.

He felt something hit the back of his ankle.

"A little help?" a female voice asked from behind.

Baker turned and saw her. She was black—light-skinned—with light brown eyes and flowing, dark brown hair. Her dress was cut to reveal her figure and if that wasn't enough, Baker could smell her even though there was some distance between them. Baker was stunned by her inherent, effortless beauty.

"Uh, yeah," he stammered.

"Well, you have to bend down and pick up the Frisbee."

"Right."

He bent down and scooped up the disc, keeping his eyes on her the entire time. She held her hands open, and he flicked the Frisbee over to her. She clapped both hands onto it.

"Thanks," she said, before turning around.

"No problem," Baker said, birds chirping all around him.

The woman went back to her friends and their game. Baker eyed the group; when he realized that there were a few guys in it, he acknowledged a wave of possessiveness, just like when he was a child and a friend had something—a toy or a video game—that he coveted. He quickly shook these thoughts loose and recognized the absurdity of feeling possessive of someone he didn't even know.

But now he couldn't leave the area that provided a view of her. He also didn't want to be perceived as some kind of weirdo-stalker. He walked on but turned to look at her every five feet or so. He had never seen someone that beautiful. Sandra caught up to Baker on the far side of the courtyard and tapped him on his shoulder.

"Hey there, stud," she said.

Baker turned around.

"What? Huh?"

"I saw you from inside," Sandra said. "A mother sees all."

"You don't know what you're talking about."

"Oh? Why don't you go talk to her?"

"Talk to who?"

"The girl in the dress," Sandra said, pulling her sunglasses off her eyes. She squinted at the group playing Frisbee in the distance. "Let me see if I know her."

Baker pulled his mom away, forcing her to walk.

"Stop, Mom! Seriously!"

"What? She's cute. But I don't know her, James. This is a big school. Looks like if you want to get to know her, you'll have to do it the old-fashioned way."

He watched her again as she threw the Frisbee and stopped to catch her breath after darting to catch an errant throw. She had long legs and strong thighs, the look of an athlete.

"You talked all that noise in the car about taking on challenges," Sandra said. "Well, here you go."

Amid the taunts, Baker knew his mother was right. He took a deep breath and started in the direction of the group.

"Give me a little space," he said. "I may talk to her, or I may not but I sure as hell am not gonna do it with you standing here."

"Meet me in front of the science building in about an hour," Sandra called at his back.

Baker heard his mother but didn't respond. He needed to focus on the serious business at hand. As he neared the group, he could hear its internal laughs and taunts. She didn't see him at first because he was out of her line of vision. He stepped into it confidently, and she saw him.

When she recognized that he was there for her, she extricated herself from the game and jogged over. Baker decided that he liked her even more for this—that she too was not afraid to take a chance.

"Hey," she said.

"Hi."

"What's up?"

"I wanted to introduce myself."

She nodded confidently. "Okay, what's your name?"

"James, but everyone calls me Baker."

Baker noticed the definition of her arm and leg muscles with the closer look. "What's your name?" he asked.

"Tiffany."

"Nice to meet you, Tiffany," he said, putting his hand out.

Tiffany took his hand and shook it firmly.

"Well, aren't you gonna say that it's nice to meet me?"

"I'm not sure if that's true or not yet," she said.

"Do you go to school here?"

"Duh." Her nostrils flared and her cheeks developed a little rosiness in them. Baker realized that she was nervous too.

"You, uh, wanna take a walk?" he asked, going for it.

She eyed him. Her light, inquisitive eyes almost looked like those of a child's whose face loved the camera. Baker remembered a girl in his fifth grade class with eyes like that.

"Sure," she said. "Wait up a moment."

Tiffany ran back to where her friends were and slipped a pair of sandals onto her feet. She returned to Baker and the two of them began walking away from the courtyard together, back toward the student center.

"Are you a freshman?" Baker asked.

"Yeah, is it that obvious?" she replied.

"Oh no. I didn't mean it like that. I just can tell that you're young."

"What about you?"

"Me? I'm actually still in high school."

Tiffany's demeanor remained the same after Baker's revelation.

"My mom teaches here. We're just hanging out today because I have a day off from football."

"You play?"

"Yeah. I play wide receiver on Churchill."

"Churchill?" she asked.

"Yeah, it's a school down here. Are you from San Antonio?"

"Nah. I'm from Dallas. I went to a high school with a good football team up there. Good, but not great. But I played sports myself. Three years on the varsity basketball team."

"I knew it," he said. "I could tell you were an athlete."

Tiffany put her hand on her hips and questioned Baker with her eyes. "How?"

"I can just tell. You move confidently—like an athlete."

She smiled.

"Plus you have those long legs."

Baker smiled genuinely, and though the comment was daring, Tiffany accepted the compliment with a shake of her head. A smile told Baker that he hadn't crossed any lines.

"Are you down here playing on the team?" he asked.

"Nope," she said. "My playing days are over. I'm just here to get an education."

They continued walking; instead of going into the student center, they walked around it and through campus.

"Let me just, I mean, can I just ask you something?" Baker asked after a few moments of silence between Tiffany and him. She was startled only because of the abruptness of his speech.

"Would you have a problem going out with someone who was still in high school?" he asked.

"What do you mean by 'go out'?"

Baker took another deep breath and stared into Tiffany's eyes. He could feel himself getting lost in them. He was sure that she felt something too. She seemed to like his confidence, perhaps because it was legitimate confidence, not that swaggering, self-important forgery of confidence that's often mistaken for self-aware cockiness. His sureness—about her, about the moment—was a turn-on as well. Tiffany had been in college a month and a lot of the guys there, even the upperclassmen, weren't as put together as Baker.

"When I first laid eyes on you, I just had to know you," Baker said. "That sounds kind of crazy, but, damn. I guess I'm asking if you'd like to hang out?"

Tiffany watched him with a wondrous look in her eyes. "Yeah. I mean, yes," she said, gathering her composure. "I would like that."

"Cool," Baker said, his lips unfurling, elongating into an ear-to-ear smile. "I have a game this coming Friday night. Will you come?"

"Sure," she said, gazing back with admiring eyes. "You have such a nice smile."

They started on their way back to the courtyard. Baker took Tiffany's hand and squeezed it. He couldn't believe that something this good could happen to him on a day that started out so bad.

When they came back around to her friends, the group was still playing Frisbee, though with less intensity than when Tiffany was part of the game. Tiffany introduced Baker to the rest of her friends, who each regarded him with kindness. Even the other males in the group extended hands out to him. Baker pulled Tiffany aside again because it was time for him to meet back up with his mother.

"I gotta go," he said, unable to peel his eyes away from hers. He could already tell that this was going to be a difficult habit to break. "I don't want to leave, but my mom and I don't get a lot of time to hang out. I don't want to disappoint her."

"I respect that, Baker," she said. "I like a guy who's close to his family. I'm very close to mine."

"I'll see you Friday night, then?"

"I'll be there," she said. "I'll be the one cheering loudly every time you make a play."

Baker smiled, turned around, and took two steps. He stopped in his tracks and walked back over to where Tiffany stood.

"You know what?" he said. "My mom can wait. You wanna grab something to eat?"

"Yes."

Tiffany and Baker walked into the UTSA's student center, and she led him to the basement level where the food court was. After ordering Mexican food, they sat down at a table near what looked to be a game room. The clicks and clacks from an air hockey game peppered the space around them. Even though he loved Mexican food, Baker's plate was left untouched as Tiffany dug into hers. But it wasn't the noisiness around him that took his attention; Baker couldn't focus on his food because he was too fixated on the woman sitting in front of him.

His episode in the morning felt like ancient history. And if there was anything to learn from it, it was that Baker didn't want to do anything to jeopardize his enjoyment of Tiffany—her face, her scent, the curves of her body. He needed all of his senses to take her in.

They finished eating and walked back upstairs, holding hands.

When they reached Tiffany's friends—still hanging out in the courtyard—Baker wrapped his arms around Tiffany's waist, interlacing his fingers behind her back.

She breathed deeply and her face flushed slightly. Baker leaned in hard and she accepted him. They kissed—one kiss—for a long time. Baker wasn't going to be the one who pulled back. Tiffany didn't volunteer for the job either. They finally did pull away, but it was more a function of needing air. Tiffany's friends had been watching the entire time, and it wasn't until she turned around to their stares that her flush deepened.

"I never do this," she said before beginning, "I mean, this is the first time I have ever kissed a guy on a first date. Well, I don't even know if this was a date or what, but, anyway, I don't know what I'm saying."

"It was a date," Baker said.

They exchanged phone numbers and Baker lingered a little while longer.

"Friday it is," he said.

"Until Friday, Baker."

They kissed—softer—three more times before Baker left and walked through the student center. He walked like a big man on campus, and it wasn't even his campus. The science building was all the way on the other end of the school's grounds and Baker used the entire time to think about this new woman. Sandra was standing out front of the science building with a smile that was less buddy-buddy than maternal.

"Mom," Baker said. "What do I do?"

"Do? What do you mean? You *did* enough. Tiffany's coming to the game Friday, right? You have her phone number, correct?"

"Yeah. But I . . . "

Baker trailed off and Sandra examined her son in the passenger seat. His eyes held puppy love in them. Her son was in love—there was not a doubt in her mind. And to a college girl, no less.

"I really like Tiffany," Baker said, finishing his thought after the pensive moment.

Sandra was not one to go easy when there was a joke to be made, even if it came at the expense of her own. Baker knew this and anticipated further ribbing. She put on her mother face, however, extracting even the faintest hint of sarcasm that might've shone through.

"It's okay, James. She likes you too. She wouldn't have agreed to see you if she didn't."

"I know all that. I just don't want to make any wrong moves with her."

"First of all, it's perfectly fine if Tiffany sees the imperfections in you. That's what love is, son," Sandra said, with down-tempo jazz coming out of the car's speakers.

"What you mean, that's what love is?" Baker asked. "Imperfection?"

"Yes. That's what it's about. You don't have to be perfect for someone to love you. You just have to be perfect for that person."

Baker looked to his mother and did not speak. He seemed to understand.

"You're gonna be fine, son. You have a good head on your shoulders and a good heart. Just be yourself. That's all I'm saying."

"Thanks, Mom."

"Now where do you want to go?" she asked. "The rest of the day is yours."

Baker looked out the window and could only think of Tiffany. His ability to daydream about her, combined with the knowledge that his daydreams would soon materialize into the real thing, comforted him in a way that he had never experienced before. Baker was long in answering Sandra because he was in love. There was no doubt about it in his mind.

"Oh, I don't know," he said, finally, his eyes still

on the road just past the windshield. The sun was beginning to creep below a tree line in the distance. "Anything sounds good right about now."

Sandra smiled and stared straight ahead, her eyes on the road as well; she had done what she set out to do—get her son out of the house, off the football field, and into the world.

7

Baker woke up to a surprise on Monday morning. It was not a bad one—no remnant of the horrific morning he'd had the day before. No. His cell phone rang before his wake-up alarm for school chimed. It was his father in California.

"Hello?" Baker said.

"Hi, son," Harold said. "Did I wake you?"

Baker shifted to the upright position in his bed. He rubbed at his eyes and cleared his throat. "No. It's okay, Dad. I have to be up for school anyway."

"How are you feeling, son?"

Baker wondered briefly if his mother had told

his father about her conversation with Nathan. But Baker wasn't going to bring it up and put it out into the universe. "I'm okay," he said.

"I'm happy for you, son. Your mother said that football is working out for you, and I just wanted to tell you that I'm proud of the kind of young man you've grown up to be."

"Thanks, Dad."

"I'm gonna be in next month to see you play."

Baker held the phone by his ear and could not speak. His father, though faraway geographically, still held a serious place in Baker's heart. He had never seen him play. Baker's low standing on past teams had released Harold from having to place his son's athletics high on the list of father-son priorities.

"Son? You there?"

"Yeah, Dad."

"I love you."

"I love you too." Baker hung up the phone and got out of bed with a clear focus, one that if he could only replicate each morning he got out of bed, the world would be his.

• •

When he got off the phone with his father, he thought of Tiffany, placing her first on his list of priorities, with football, surprisingly, not even entering his mind. In fact, Baker had fought the urge to call or text Tiffany on Sunday evening after he and Sandra got home from a movie, but he knew he should exert some self-control. He'd left the theater with the plan to call Tiffany after practice on Monday.

School was a breeze in those early days of the school year because of football. Players were given room to goof off or even sleep in class if they wished. The administrators helped the players' causes by turning a blind eye to any minor issue. Forester never heard a word about any of his players being slackers. Even non-players received some fringe benefits from the teachers' and administrators' obsession with Churchill's early season push for state.

Baker, however, continued to pay attention in class and to do his school work conscientiously. Sandra's advice to take his studies seriously always rested in the back of his mind, no matter what kind of inroads he made on the football field. This day held a little more weight, though, with question marks all around. He wasn't sure if he'd be cleared to practice. As a result, he wasn't sure about his grip on a starting wide-receiver spot. He quieted his mind as best he could by studying extra hard that day—probably more than any other player on the team. He'd get all the answers to his questions after final bell.

The locker room was alive with the energy of a new season, a nervous kind of feeling born of the expectations that come with Texas high school football, mingled with the hope that the team would perform well. Churchill had won three playoff games the season before, and in the closed world of Texas, where everything is analyzed in a vacuum, anything less than Churchill getting at least one round further in the state playoffs than the season before would be looked upon as a failure, even with all of the graduated starters.

The expectations in the San Antonio community were very real, as Forester and his players were well aware. It was no coincidence that the message written on the blackboard in the locker room was, "Move ahead or don't move at all." Sure it was reductive, and maybe a little macabre, but Forester wanted his players to know that the world was a cruel and unforgiving place. He also wanted them to know and understand that expectations were a good thing. And he wanted them to know it on the first Monday before the first game under the Friday night lights.

Baker didn't really need the reminder to do his best. Sandra had always placed expectations at the neck of her son. They weren't specific in Baker's case. She didn't push ideas of academic or athletic grandeur on him. She had simply wanted him to care, to give a hoot. She didn't really worry about what specifically captured her son's attention and time.

Nathan came out of his office and scanned the locker room. When his eyes rested on Baker, they flashed. He nodded for the wide receiver to come over and join him.

Baker stood up and walked across the locker room. He passed by small groups of conversing teammates. Other teammates sat alone and listened to music with closed eyes.

"Close the door," Nathan said.

After closing the door Baker immediately noticed the dead silence inside the trainer's room. Nathan's office held the tone of a funeral parlor even when there was no current malady to discuss. Baker wanted out of this place.

"How did it go yesterday?"

Baker recalled the first time he woke up on Sunday morning, but was careful not to let any of its residue show on his face. He wondered if Nathan somehow knew and waited anxiously a beat, but his trainer simply waited patiently for Baker's response.

"It was fine. I stayed off my feet for the most part. Just went out with my mom for a little while."

"No symptoms, whatsoever?"

"Uh-uh."

"Good."

Nathan took down some information on his clipboard and then looked back up at Baker.

"I'm gonna clear you for today's practice with no restrictions. But I'll be out there watching you. If you experience any shortness of breath or any other symptoms, let me know."

"Will do. Thanks."

"No problem."

Baker left the gloomy place and hoped never to set foot in there again. He knew that would be impossible now that he was actually setting foot on the field as a frontline player. With the question about whether or not he could practice answered,

Baker hurried to get changed into his uniform and see about his starting position.

. . . .

Ripley pulled Baker aside before the official start of practice, and they ran through some routes. If this was any indication, Baker still owned a starting spot. Ripley wouldn't have wasted his time if he were not one of the team's starters at the wide-receiver position. Baker didn't ask Ripley if that was the case because he wanted to focus on the work.

Saturday's scrimmage felt light-years away. He had some rust to knock off before the first game.

Churchill's passing attack was fairly sophisticated by high school standards, with most of the complicated reads and adjustments falling on Ripley's shoulders. The QB's experience allowed the team to do interesting things with play designs and route combinations. His strong arm was the golden key to all this, of course. His ability to drive the ball down the field allowed for a healthy dose of deep passing plays in the game plan.

"Out of this formation, a lot of teams like to blitz," Ripley said to Baker. "They'll bring pressure off the strong side edge. You gotta see that early and then break off your route. Otherwise, I get hammered."

"I know," Baker said. "If I see the blitz, I have to show you my eyes."

"That's right. Let's do one of those."

Baker got set to the right of the formation and imagined that an entire defense was lined up across from Ripley and him. Ripley called out a dialed down cadence—complete with blitz pickup instructions—and made eye contact with Baker. He patted the ball and dropped back to pass. Baker shot out of his stance and snapped his head around to Ripley. He cut off his intended route, sitting down in the vacated area as a hot-read blitz adjustment. When Ripley saw Baker, he threw an accurate dart to him.

Baker ran back over to Ripley with the ball.

"Good," Ripley said. "We'll do some of those in practice so you can see it live. A lot of times, teams will blitz early to try to scare us out of passing deep." Ripley smiled. "But we're not scared of teams that blitz because my receivers and I are *always* on the same page."

Baker nodded and shook Ripley's hand. He was now one of Ripley's receivers—someone to be trusted and respected. His retention of the offense was sharp as he and Ripley ran through the pre-practice series of plays.

"Coach is coming," Ripley said with nod. "Good work."

The coaching staff converged around the team as Forester stepped onto the field. There weren't any words or speeches given to enhance the focus of the team. For the players who had been at Churchill, it was time to get ready for the real games. For newcomers to the varsity level, it was time to observe and learn how to do it the right way.

Baker was focused and ready to put the injury

blip behind him. On the field, there was no time to worry about injury. It would be dangerous for him to do so, and he would hurt the team if he did. Before Forester blew the first whistle that represented the beginning of practice, Baker relaxed and decided to put the hit from the scrimmage completely out of his mind. He did not want to play scared.

Churchill's pace was crisp as practice periods started and ended to the tweets from Forester's whistle. The execution was sharp as well—Ripley didn't have one pass touch the ground during one-on-one and seven-on-seven portions of practice. On one seven-on-seven rep, Baker caught a seam route for a touchdown, down the left hash. When he turned around, Whitlock was the first player in the end zone to celebrate the big play. Whitlock's ankle looked fine to Baker, and he had no limp. Baker hadn't seen Whitlock taking extra rest during practice. This further reassured Baker that rest and treatment were the keys to staying strong on the football field, though a rogue thought also picked at him, causing him to wonder if he had done the right thing in not being vocal about his strange Sunday morning symptoms.

"Okay, last rep!" Forester shouted.

The final play of the seven-on-seven called for Baker to run the twenty-yard dig, or in-cut. This was the same route that he took the shot on at the end of the scrimmage. He needed to feel success with this play on the practice field so that he could envision it during a game. The coaches needed this visual evidence too.

The play was a slow developing one, designed to beat a zone defense. When Baker saw zone before the snap of the ball, he knew the play would have a chance. He got upfield as fast as could and at twelve yards, peeked inside to see where the free safety was. He saw that the defender had taken a bad angle—the in-cut would be there. He cut inside at twenty yards and made his way across the field. Ripley released the pass, leaving it out in front just a tad, in an effort to hit Baker in stride.

Baker saw the ball coming at him clearly. He

tracked it and stuck his arms out. It made a suction-like sound as it slapped against his gloves. The ball did hit him in stride, which was a good thing because the recovering free safety would've tattooed him with an inaccurate throw from Ripley. He heard the safety whiff, and the sound of it—the rush—was like a gust of wind in his ear. He escaped the middle of the field with the ball and his body in one piece and then took the ball to the end zone, untouched.

The elusive harmony of football was on full display during that play. One second too late and you have destruction. If everything is on time, you have beauty. Baker shook his head in the end zone. He was happy about the result of the play, but also knew that he was playing with an unpredictable wild fire, and in truth, it scared him a little. Ever since the hit, there was a hyper-awareness that any moment on the football field could be his last. He wasn't going to play scared though and shook the negative and heavy thoughts out of his head, like a quarterback shakes off a bad throw into double-coverage.

By Wednesday it was cemented. Baker was set to start at receiver for Churchill's first game of the season. Forester never said anything to him officially—no congratulation or affirmation of his status on the squad. The proof came from Baker lining up with the first string during drills at the end of Wednesday's team practice period.

Hayes came by Baker's locker after Wednesday's practice to give him the news, just for good measure. To Hayes, Baker's ascension on the depth chart was a win as momentous as any from his own playing days. Baker meant that much to Hayes. Baker was a true representation of what a good attitude and hard work could accomplish.

In true Baker style, he did not celebrate at the news of securing a starting spot. His mother wasn't even the first to know. No, someone else got that honor.

"Hello?" Tiffany answered after two rings.

She and Baker had had three calls already that week, but rarely discussed football.

"I did it," Baker said into the receiver. "Coach Hayes let me know after practice."

"Congratulations!" Tiffany squealed.

"Thank you. Thank you."

"I'll be there," Tiffany said. "Who do you guys play?"

"Clark," Baker said. "They're from San Antonio."

Earlier over the phone, they had agreed to hang out Friday night after the game without making any specific plans. Tiffany knew the result of the game would dictate the mood afterward. Seeing Tiffany would be enough for Baker.

"I'm gonna let my mom know," Baker said. "Can I call you later?"

"Sure."

"Okay. Bye, Tiffany."

"Bye, Baker."

Sandra would also be in the stands for Baker's

first game of the season. She knew the game enough to understand the basic differences between winning and losing teams. Sandra did not, however, know the first thing about Baker's position because as a spot player, he had never explained it before. Now that he was a starter, it was time to give his mother a tutorial on the responsibilities and goals of the wide-receiver position regarding winning football. Baker gave his mother the detailed, albeit quick, tutorial with pure joy and enthusiasm. He shared the difficulty in getting across a cornerback's face on a slant route and the courage and strength it took to go into the box to dig out a hulking linebacker. This education happened on the eve of the first game of the season at the dinner table. Sandra watched her son with reverence. His passion for this game—foreign in her eyes—was no longer a mystery.

Baker left his mother at the kitchen table and went upstairs to a night filled with justified tossing and turning. Surprisingly, she too had trouble sleeping the night before the first game of Churchill's season. Sandra couldn't wait to see her son go to work.

8

A NEW SEASON ALWAYS BROUGHT ABOUT FEELINGS of optimism, which, in turn, generated enthusiasm. Baker had so many reasons to be excited that the lone negative thought—the threat of head-related injury—was pushed aside by the brighter things. He was ready to explode onto the Texas high school football radar. After this night, James Baker would be known outside of the walls and practice fields of Churchill High School.

School was a breeze—a sham of a day, where everything—math, history, even Spanish—was football related. Baker kept the storm inside of him steady and brewing. He had heard stories of players getting too riled up long before the official act. Baker knew that it wouldn't happen to him if he controlled it. He believed that his mind was strong enough.

So there he was a couple of hours before kickoff, in the locker room, getting his mind right. Tiffany texted with a good luck message, along with an ode to how much she missed him. This, surprisingly, didn't bring any additional nerves. Football and Tiffany were separate for Baker. Church and state. Sandra's lecture on love was still fresh in Baker's mind. According to her, Tiffany's presence in his life was the proverbial cherry on top; she'd like Baker for who he was, not for what he did on the field.

Forester walked into the locker an hour before the game. He sent the specialists—long snapper, holder, kickers, and returners—out to warm up. Baker couldn't tell if his coach, Forester, was any more focused for the first game of the season because he always held the same steely expression on his face. He was a hard man to gauge because of his rocky exterior. But Forester did go to greet each player, one by one, at his respective locker. Baker didn't recall Forester doing this the season before, so perhaps this was an example of his coach evolving.

When Forester reached Baker's locker, he smiled and held his hand out. "Have a hell of a night, Baker," he said. "You've earned this."

"Thanks, Coach."

Forester moved on, and Baker took his helmet and hit the field. The stands were already filled some forty-five minutes before kickoff. Baker allowed himself a minute to take it all in. The night was perfect. *Three deep breaths and one more look all around*, Baker thought. After that, he went over to the backup QB and caught some passes. It didn't take long for him to get a lather. His muscles were loose because of the thorough pregame stretch administered to him by Nathan's assistant. As kickoff neared, Baker felt the anticipation. *This* was why he played, why he put himself through those workouts during the summer. He remembered the beauty in football as he gathered up everything inside of himself in preparation of lighting the fuse. Football was a beautiful mess, a sweet and poisonous brew of contradiction.

Ripley walked over to Baker and shook his hand.

"You're my guy, Bake," Ripley said. "Show me your eyes on those hots. I'm gonna put the passes right on you. All you gotta do is make one guy miss and take it home."

"I got you," Baker said.

"You nervous?"

"Hell no."

"You got a girl up there somewhere?" Ripley asked, as they stared up at the throng, not an empty spot in the bleachers now.

"I do. She's up there somewhere. Two actually," Baker said, with a chuckle. "My mom is here too."

They shook again.

"Show 'em," Ripley said.

Baker and the rest of the team ran back into the locker room for the final time before kickoff. Forester liked to bring his team back into the locker room right before kickoff so his players could sit in silence for a few minutes. Football, itself, is loud enough, Forester always thought.

9

CHURCHILL'S OFFENSE TOOK THE FIELD FIRST AMID the gathering drone of its home crowd. The buzz was palpable, as if one could reach out, grab it, and stuff it into their pocket. Baker whispered a mantra to himself—"Be fast, be decisive"—before joining his first ever regular season huddle as a starter. Ripley barked out the kind of play that lets the opposing team know that you're not kidding around: an all-go route combination with Baker as the primary receiver. His job was simple. If there was press coverage in front him, he would have to beat the jam, get downfield, and create separation. If Clark High's defense employed a zone coverage, Baker would have to eat up the cushion and then get downfield.

The huddle clapped as one, and Baker took his spot at the end of the line on the right side. Ripley got under center and scanned Clark's hulking defense. The defenders were big and strong, but Ripley wanted to see about their collective speed. He saw some things on tape that pointed to Churchill's speedy, skill position players—namely Baker and Whitlock—giving Clark's defense trouble.

Baker looked inside before the snap. There was an eerie calm down there on the field, as if the crowd noise hovered over the field at a certain height and didn't come down to cross the threshold. The field was for players only. All the rest of it—the crowd, the boosters, the scouts, even the coaches—did not matter. Baker liked this feeling. This feeling was what he played for.

Ripley took the snap and dropped back fast. Pressure came from both edges. Baker beat the press coverage off the line, yet the corner was long enough and possessed a stride that was fluid enough to make up the distance. Baker hugged the hash mark and turned on his jets. The corner strode as long as his gangly limbs allowed, until Baker kicked it into another gear. The gap widened. Baker threw his hand up into the air. Before the two defensive ends could converge and make Ripley into a sandwich, the quarterback stepped up into the pocket with his eyes set firmly downfield.

Baker flashed. Ripley bombed it down the right sideline as far as he could. The ends smashed him just as he let go of the ball. Baker tracked the arc of the football. It would be out in front of him. He put his head down to squeeze out the last ounce of speed from his legs. When he looked up again, the ball was gone. Looking down he saw the ball was nestled between his hands. As he squeezed it tighter and kept moving, all around him seemed draped in silence. Then he was in the end zone and the referee raised both arms in the air. The play was an eighty-yard touchdown—Baker's first varsity touchdown on the first play from scrimmage. It was all woven together in fragments, like a dream. He handed the ball back to the ref and all sound returned.

Churchill's players—save Ripley, who needed to be peeled off the turf—mobbed Baker on the sidelines. The crowd noise was deafening. Baker was a number-one receiver, a true playmaker.

· ·

The score was fourteen to ten, Churchill over Clark, after one quarter. Baker had two more long catches on Churchill's second scoring drive, capped off by a six-yard touchdown run by Whitlock. The second quarter began with Forester laying into his defense on the sidelines. Baker watched the harangue out of the corner of his eye as Clark kicked the ball back to Churchill.

"Wake up!" Forester yelled at his embattled troops. "We covered all of this during the week! The curl, with the post going behind! Details! De-tails!"

Baker then turned all the way around to watch the reaction of the defense. Each member of the unit was attentive, watching Forester as he spoke, with a few of the guys dipping their heads at certain moments.

"Your minds need to be clear out there! If you're not thinking straight, we'll get someone out there who is! Wake the hell up!"

Forester stomped away from the deflated unit. The more empathetic position coaches approached the wounded players to restore their confidence and focus. Baker took the field with the offense where it would begin its third drive of the game at its own thirty-yard line. Ripley pulled Baker aside before they joined the huddle.

"Look out for mixed coverages on this drive," Ripley said. "They won't go straight man-to-man defense on us anymore. Your speed is too much."

"They started throwing out some zone the last drive."

"Good," Ripley said. "Find the soft spots and I'll hit you."

Ripley called the play and broke the huddle. Whitlock was back in after taking a drive off. Churchill's coaches liked to ease Whitlock into the season slowly because of the cumulative punishment he'd take throughout.

"Red, fifty-two!" Ripley called out. "Red fifty-two! Set, hut!"

The ball was snapped, and Ripley dropped back for a pass. Churchill's offensive line dropped into pass sets as well. Whitlock waited, readying for pass protection. At the last moment, Ripley handed the ball off to Whitlock. The draw play was a new addition to Churchill's offensive package, meant to take advantage of an opponent's tendency to focus on Ripley and the passing game.

As Whitlock took the ball he saw a gaping hole to his right. He hit it and reached the second level of Clark's defense. Baker influenced his man upfield and then locked onto him. Whitlock made the strong-side linebacker miss and burst his way down the right sideline.

Baker held his block, pumping his legs into the ground like pistons. The defender was powerless against Baker's relentlessness as Baker drove him off the field of play and into Churchill's sideline. Meanwhile, Whitlock was down the right sideline and into the end zone. The seventy-yard touchdown run would not have been possible if not for Baker's block. The play would've gone for thirty yards or so had Baker not been so inclined to put his body on the line. *That* was the kind of play that made an offense dangerous—big play potential at any turn, whether through the air or on the ground. The potential for virtuosity on even the most basic of plays. Whitlock was a genius out on the football field and Ripley an artist. But Baker was the one who brought it all together—the proverbial glue, or better yet, the glue gun.

Forester allowed himself to smile as he witnessed Baker help the defender up from the ground on Churchill's sideline. The touchdown was nice, but it wasn't the thing that excited Forester most. Baker excited him: his actions and his sportsmanship. *Baker*, he thought, *he's the missing piece.*

The sideline converged on Baker after he sent the Clark defender back to his own sideline with a pat on the rear. Whitlock jumped onto Baker's back, placing a literal interpretation atop the symbolic happenings.

"You put that boy in Mexico!" Whitlock yelled, clutching onto Baker's shoulders.

Churchill's crowd swelled at the sight of the enthusiasm of its players. The fans loved to see the players enjoying themselves like that. It went beyond the vicarious. The players were them, but on an elevated level. The stadium rocked and rocked until the kickoff allowed for a moment to breathe. Everyone had to remember to breathe.

Forester walked over to Baker after his teammates dispersed. He put a bulging bicep around his player. The coach didn't look much like the other coaches in Texas. He was impressive and imposing. Baker looked up at Forester.

"Hey, that's the way to play the game and *that's* the way to respect your opponent." Forester patted Baker on the back of the helmet.

"Thanks, Coach."

They parted. Forester was different. The game mattered to him. But it wasn't the only thing that mattered. He wanted his players at Churchill to learn something from the game—that football could impact their lives in a positive way, and shape them as men. Baker agreed; there were lessons to learn from the game.

When the defense took the field, Baker had a moment to catch his breath. He looked up into the stands and wondered where his special fans were. Other than the people in the first several rows, the faces blended together to make a wall, from which only sound could be recognized. He knew his mother wouldn't be one to sit right up front anyway. Sandra would've preferred the eagle-eye view to see the whole thing.

As for Tiffany, he didn't know her well enough to

assume at what vantage point she preferred watching a game. He couldn't spot her in the rows right behind Churchill's sideline, so he stopped looking. By the time Baker turned his attention back to the field, Clark's offense had driven the ball to Churchill's twenty-yard line. The defense struggled with Clark's power running game, and that was not a good sign. Even with the universal shift to the spread offense out of the pistol formation, the main staple of Texas football remained smash mouth, power-running football.

Early on, it looked to be that Churchill's offense would have to carry the load, but the run defense would have to get fixed.

Clark ran the ball into the end zone, and the score was twenty to seventeen after the extra point. Churchill's crowd was silenced by the bullying approach of Clark's offense. Nothing is more demoralizing than when a team runs the ball right at you. Forester didn't address the defense after the latest score it had given up. He had said what he wanted to say earlier. True improvement against the run would only come after a tough week of practice, and a quick fix would not be in the works. Churchill's defense simply needed to survive the second half.

The offense took possession of the ball with one timeout, and a minute left before halftime. The team's kicker was reliable. Fifty yards would put it in range for a realistic field goal attempt. Ripley received three plays on the sideline. That way, he could get the unit into hurry-up mode and direct the offense without huddling.

The first play of the drive brought a successful slant route to the left side that got things started. Churchill's offensive players knew the next two plays and lined up right as the ref spotted the ball. Baker saw that Clark's defense was backed up in a conservative prevent zone, protecting against the big play. He would have a free release off the line of scrimmage, and the healthy cushion would set up the deep dig route as the perfect call. That was the call, in fact, and Churchill's offense needed to hit the route if it wanted a real chance at three points before the end of the half.

Ripley took the snap; there wasn't much pressure and the coverage was a basic cover-two shell. Baker accelerated and got downfield. He eyed the strong safety, a must when running in-breaking routes. The safety was where he should have been in that defensive alignment and not too much of a threat. Baker reached his eighteen-yard landmark and broke inside. Ripley released the pass, a low one that would give Baker a chance for a safe catch. As the ball neared Baker, he bent down to catch it, but when he did, the strong safety clipped him from behind. The fast-approaching free safety flashed and caught Baker low, and with helmet-to-helmet contact. There wasn't a loud sound, like during the scrimmage, but the shot was clean. Baker held on, but his mind dropped out for a moment as his body hit the field.

As quickly as the hit occurred, he came to just as fast, opening his eyes, and seeing dark sky above. Baker lifted himself up to his feet and with every ounce of resolve in his body, stood firm and buried the fog. His head was tapped during the play. He noticed the loss of sound and the blurred vision, but his legs held firm. He could perceive Ripley gyrating for the offense to get lined up for a spike. Baker took his place as the ref spotted the ball.

After his catch, Churchill needed only a few more yards for the field goal attempt. Baker couldn't hear Ripley's cadence and had to rely on the movement around him instead. Luckily, Ripley went to the other side on the next play and completed a pass for ten yards. After calling its final timeout Churchill trotted out its kicker with six seconds left.

Baker put his hands on his knees, but had the wherewithal to exaggerate his breathing. He was not tired or winded; his physical shape was in peak form. He had made a show of being tired because he wanted to take attention away from his head shot. His thinking was clear enough to do that anyway. Ripley approached during the timeout and put a hand on Baker's back.

"You alright, Bake?"

Baker heard his quarterback, but the sound was muffled.

"Yeah," he said, gasping histrionically. "Just winded. Gotta catch my breath."

Ripley walked off the field with Baker. By the time they reached the sidelines, Baker's vision was partially restored, with incandescent filament explosions in his peripheries. There was an acuteness to his movements, a conscious perception to them. And he didn't dare test his body yet.

This isn't going to be easy, he thought. But no one from the staff—not Nathan, Forester, nor Coach Hayes—came over to check up on him. The hit had been low and without a sickening, plastic-on-plastic clap on impact. Perhaps his phony show of fatigue had worked in hiding its significance from his coaches. Baker's busy first half reinforced the notion.

Churchill's kicker knocked the ball through the uprights, and the team went up twenty-three to seventeen over Clark.

Baker did not look up at the kick, but instead relied on the fan reaction behind him. His hearing was slowly coming back. His focus expanded like sunrise, bringing everything to life inside of him. He had no time to feel sorry for himself as he walked off the field for halftime. He needed to focus on hiding the possibility that he may have suffered a full-blown concussion this time.

Halftime was a blur for Baker, though not only because his head was throbbing. The coaches rushed to put forth adjustments that players from both sides of the ball may or may not have grasped. Baker was a lucky one; he knew the playbook inside-out, so the coaches didn't feel the need to grill him up close. Baker did watch Nathan throughout the break as the trainer was busy tending to Whitlock's fragile ankle. Baker made sure to steer clear. It was then that Baker realized that *he* was the one in control of the narrative. As long as he could control his mind, he'd be able to stay out on the field.

After the twelve minutes were up, and it was time to go back on the field for the second half, Baker stood up slowly. He didn't want to tempt the nausea in his stomach to rise up and blow his cover. He stood tall, slowly elongating his spine to its full height, and the nausea wasn't there, lurking in the dark alley that was his mind. He walked into the restroom and looked straight into the mirror. He could hear his teammates behind him, their war-cries stirring and then solidifying into one. His eyes were foggy, even he could see that. Yet there was no nausea, no threat of vomiting. *I can make this work*, Baker thought. *I'm not ready to get off the field yet.*

* * *

Clark received the kickoff to open the second half and drove seventy-two yards to take the lead, twenty-four to twenty-three. With his vision and hearing back, along with a small yet nagging headache above his left eye, Baker took the field with the starting offense, midway through the third quarter, with Churchill trailing for the first time.

The second-half plan was to pound Whitlock against Clark's defense. The reasoning was twofold: first, Churchill's defense needed a break to catch its breath, and second, Forester wanted to keep Clark's defense off balance. That wouldn't be possible if the opposing defenders were teeing off on Ripley and Churchill's passing game. Feeding the ball to Whitlock was just fine by Baker. He felt able to fulfill his duty on each play, but given his condition, run blocking was more doable than running routes.

The first play of the drive was a simple dive play to the left. Baker barely had any contact on the play, and Whitlock ran for a gain of eleven. As Baker ran back to the huddle, the pressure in his skull mounted. He told himself to breathe above all, thinking that if he could just focus on that simple task, he could push through the pain. Second down was a big play for Churchill. Ripley tossed the ball to Whitlock on a sweep going right. This was a play that Churchill's coaching staff devised as a way to take advantage of Baker's physical blocking ability. Knowing he wasn't able to block with force, Baker used body position and timing to block his man.

When Whitlock took the pitch, there was a natural alley between the strong-side tight end and Baker. If Baker could just keep his man out of the alley, Whitlock could make a long gain. Baker baited his man into taking a false step to the outside. By the time the recovering defender knew there was a sweep coming his way, it was too late. Whitlock had already hit the hole and raced downfield. Churchill's running back took it all the way to the end zone for a fifty-nine yard touchdown. Baker keyed the long run without blocking his defender, let alone laying a finger on him. Churchill was ahead again, thirty to twenty-four.

Baker joined in the elation along the Churchill sideline amid pats on the back of the helmet. With each soft blow, he squinted and braced for a dull jolt to his brain. By the time he reached the bench near the far edge of the sideline, his head was in a full-fledged daze. He didn't take his helmet off because he didn't want anyone looking into his eyes. A few seats down, Nathan was examining Whitlock's ankle. Baker's secret was safe, and though he realized he was putting his health at risk, the pull of being on the field was too much.

Churchill's defense managed to hold Clark to a field goal as time expired in the third, cutting the Chargers' lead to thirty to twenty-seven. The defense caught a lucky break in holding Clark to a field goal. One of Clark's wide receivers dropped a sure touchdown in the back of the end zone. On fourth down, Clark's head coach opted for the three points.

Forester knew that his team had to take advantage of the dropped touchdown. After the kickoff, Churchill's offense came onto the field with a challenge on its shoulders, knowing its defense would not be able to hold up if the score remained the same. A touchdown would put the game out of reach.

Ripley dropped back on the first play of the drive and looked Baker's way on an eight-yard stop route. Baker was slow getting out of his break and without time to scan other options, Ripley tucked the ball down and gained three yards. Ripley met Baker outside of the huddle before the next play.

"You okay?" Ripley asked, flames of competition in his eyes. "The corner was off. What happened with the stop?"

"My foot got caught in the turf," Baker said.

"Okay," Ripley said, "we need you now!"

Baker nodded and the two players joined the rest of the huddle. Ripley called out the play, an off-tackle run to Whitlock. Even though the play was designed to go away from Baker, he still had an important responsibility. His job was to cut off any pursuing defenders from the backside, thereby protecting Whitlock from a blind-side hit from a pursuing defender.

Ripley snapped the ball and Baker couldn't muster a burst off the line. The backside corner sliced past him and nailed an unsuspecting Whitlock as the back made his way through the hole. Whitlock nearly fumbled from the blunt-force hit to his side, making the gain of three yards an almost-disaster. To make matters worse, Whitlock limped to the sideline after aggravating his ankle on the play. The back-to-back subpar plays put Baker under the spotlight like never before.

Whereas before the hit to the head, Baker felt no pressure, now it was there and all around him. His teammates eyed him with tight lips in the huddle. Gone were congratulatory smiles borne of Baker's big plays of the recent past. Football is about the present—one play. The past did not exist on the field.

Ripley said nothing about the blown block because there was simply no time to dwell. It was third and four and Churchill badly needed a first down. After the play call, Ripley hurried the offense to the line. Baker took a deep breath as he lined up across from the cornerback. Clark's defense was in a press-man look, meaning that they had no respect for Churchill's offense with the game on the line.

Just one play, Baker thought to himself right before the snap. When Ripley took the ball and dropped back to pass, Baker beat the jam and ran right down the hash. The beaten corner recovered and carried Baker down the seam. At twenty yards, Baker broke his route inside for the post. Ripley threw it to him on a rope, somehow clearing the sinking outside linebacker.

The oncoming free safety flashed in Baker's vision; he cupped his hands together to catch the ball. His eyes closed on reflex. Baker didn't want to see the free safety clobber him; if it was going to happen, his eyes would be closed. When he opened them, he was streaking to the end zone for the game-sealing touchdown. Instead of dislodging Baker from the ball, Clark's free safety drilled his own man—the cornerback—with the crown of his helmet. Both Clark defenders lay on the turf—an eerie din descending on the stadium as they stayed motionless for a bit—before each got to a knee and shook out the cobwebs.

10

THE LONG TOUCHDOWN CATCH BY BAKER PROVED to be the difference in the game. Churchill won by the score of thirty-seven to thirty-four. Baker was mobbed by teammates, coaches, and boosters alike in the locker room. His fourth-quarter errors were long-forgotten, the winning score serving as the lasting image. He didn't know how the play happened; he remembered closing his eyes right before contact, as if the car crash was unavoidable. But he wasn't hit.

Ripley's locker was three stalls down. Baker walked over and sat down next to the quarterback.

"Hey," Baker said, "what happened on the touchdown?"

"What do you mean *happened*?"

"I mean, the safety was bearing down on me. He had me lined up and everything. How did he miss me?"

"Well," Ripley said, unrolling the tape around his swollen right wrist. "I was on the ground as you scored. Both defensive ends crushed me as I threw it. All I know is that you made the play."

Baker sighed.

"Why do you wanna know?" Ripley asked, sensing that Baker was troubled.

"I just . . . nothing. Just wondering."

Ripley shrugged. "Ask Whitlock. He was on the sideline."

Baker looked across the locker room and found Whitlock, sitting with his right leg across the perched left. He was kneading his ginger ankle.

"Whitlock?" Baker asked. "You think he's mad about the missed block?"

"Lucky? Nah. He's not like that. He knows how the game goes sometimes."

Baker walked over to Whitlock and stood in front of him. Whitlock looked up.

"What up, Bake?"

"Hey, man. I just wanted to talk to you for a minute."

"All good," he said, wincing as he rearranged his sitting position.

Baker pulled a chair in front of Whitlock and sat. "Sorry about that block, man. That was a bad hit you took."

"Aw, don't sweat it. That stuff happens to all of us," Whitlock said.

"Thanks. Can I ask you question?"

Whitlock nodded.

"You were on the sidelines for the touchdown. What happened with the safety?"

Whitlock smiled. "The safety? That boy was fittin' to crush you, and you gave this little stutter."

Baker thought about closing his eyes as the safety neared.

"And the safety hesitated for a like a spilt second," Whitlock continued. "Then he hit his own guy." He chuckled. "Lit his ass up too."

Baker watched Whitlock with intent, as if the running back's words were spoken in some alien language.

"And you," Whitlock said. "You ran into the end zone."

Baker didn't speak. The crowded locker room suddenly went silent. Baker and Whitlock were alone with their understanding of the other's fears about what the game can take from you. Whitlock, the more experienced player of the two, eyed Baker and could probably figure out the wide receiver's troubles if he tried. Baker should've been riding high after what he had just done on the field, but there was something happening inside of him.

"It's just . . . " Baker said, before looking down at the floor. "I'm just afraid, man."

"Of what?"

Tears pooled in Baker's eyes, but somehow did not fall. He knew inside that this was fleeting. A tear finally did fall down his left cheek.

Whitlock wasn't startled by his teammate's show of emotion. He was emotional himself, being one who gave his all when out on the field, to the point of crying in the locker room on several occasions of big games in the past. The only strange part for Whitlock was that Baker had cried after the first game of the season—a game that the wide receiver had dominated.

Baker wiped the tear away furtively and popped out of the chair, bolt upright. Whitlock stood up slowly and they were face to face. He leaned close to Baker.

"Talk to Coach Forester if you got something weighing on you," Whitlock said. "He's really good about things. And you know, you got brothers in this locker room too."

"Thanks, man," Baker said, before turning

abruptly and walking over to his locker. The room was thinned out now. The guys had taken their showers, changed clothes, and left. Baker went to an empty shower stall and turned on the water. He cried lightly as the hot water fell down his face. It was strange, this emotional outburst. He didn't know where it came from. The steam collected all around him as Baker leaned back against one wall of the stall. He didn't want to let go, but it was clear that the train was coming for him.

Tiffany texted Baker shortly after the game's exciting conclusion. Though she did not know Baker well, she'd felt a swell of pride in her chest as she watched him streak into the end zone. Tiffany was an athlete and knew all too well the physical demands that contact sports called for. Baker's resolve impressed her. She already knew he had a flair for the daring, and a sense of humor from their initial encounter on campus.

They had agreed to meet up outside of the locker room after Baker showered and changed. Baker had arranged for his mother to meet him there as well. He figured he'd get that part out of the way quickly. Tiffany stood next to Sandra outside of the locker room. Sandra intuited who Tiffany was, but Tiffany was unaware of Baker's connection to the woman standing next to her. Sandra smiled knowingly as the young woman next to her checked and rechecked her phone for messages. The door to the locker room opened, and Baker walked out slowly, achingly. His eyes lit up at the sight of the two women. Seeing the two of them was the elixir he needed after the night he'd had on the field. He approached.

"Hey, Mom," Baker said, before giving Sandra a hug.

Tiffany did a double take that almost snapped her neck when she realized what was happening. Then she smiled shyly. Baker then looked at Tiffany.

"Hi Tiffany," he said.

They hugged, and Tiffany stood speechless.

"This is my mom, Sandra," he said with a wave of his arm. "Mom, this is Tiffany."

The two shook hands and finally, Tiffany relaxed.

"She teaches at your school."

"Oh yeah?" Tiffany said, purely out of reflex.

Sandra smiled again and it relaxed Tiffany even more.

"So," Baker said to both women. "How did you like the game?"

Sandra looked at her son with a wide gaze.

"Wow!" she said. "That was thrilling."

"Yeah," Tiffany said. "You played an amazing game."

"Thanks," Baker said. "That was my first time ever being in the game when it was on the line. It was a rush."

Tiffany could see the emotion in Baker's eyes, and knew what he was feeling. She herself was dealing with the withdrawal of competition.

"So what shall we do?" Sandra asked.

Baker turned to Tiffany.

"You wanna eat?" he asked.

Tiffany hesitated, not so much because of Sandra's presence as Baker's confidence. He wasn't nervous about introducing her to his mother, and though staggered by the development, Tiffany found yet another thing she liked about him. "Yeah. Let's eat."

"One thing though," Baker said with a smile. "We eat vegan. Is that cool?"

"Like, vegan-vegan? No animal products at all?" Tiffany asked, with fear in her eyes.

Baker nodded and Sandra concurred.

"Sure. It'll be an experience," Tiffany said, gamely. "It's asking a lot of a girl from Dallas, but I'll try it."

The three walked into the parking lot next to the field and the space was empty. The only ghosts of attrition left were the crushed-out beer cans, caught in tire tracks. Baker let Tiffany sit up front next to his mother because Sandra had raised a gentleman. He also wanted the extra room in the back seat to stretch out his legs, which were stiffening up from all the snaps. Surprisingly, Baker's head was better. No fog. No headache. No nausea. He did his mental checklist of the symptoms and was content to put this latest episode out of his mind.

As the emotion of the game dissipated, so did Baker's dread over his penchant for taking hits to the head on the football field, though the residue surrounding the issue could never be completely cleared out of his mind.

When Sandra pulled into the parking lot of the best vegan restaurant in all of San Antonio, Baker sat in the back seat feeling confused. Confused about his future. Confused about his erratic mood. He knew one thing for certain—that when he was out on the football field, he had to play with his eyes open. The winning touchdown catch had been nice, but there was also a great deal of luck involved. As for talking to Nathan or Forester about what he was feeling, he just wasn't sure. On one hand, he had things under control in terms of paying close attention to his symptoms. He was not stupid. If things got too heavy, he would definitely talk to Nathan and Forester. For now, though, he was content to bask in the opportunity to play the game he loved at a high level.

After dinner, Sandra drove to the house and Baker picked up his car. He and Tiffany then drove to the promenade at La Cantera to catch a movie. Their decision to pass on a film was cemented when they got a look at the options available. A walk through the open-air galleria was the better option. Baker took Tiffany's hand as they walked by the different storefronts, a slight breeze at their backs.

"That was all vegan?" Tiffany exclaimed. "How do they get it to taste so good?"

"They do it with plants," Baker said with a dead-pan delivery.

"Well, yeah, duh," Tiffany replied.

The couple shared a laugh before a silence fell between them, the tenor of which was not at all uncomfortable.

Baker grabbed at his sore hamstring.

"The hamstring, huh?" Tiffany asked, knowingly.

"Yeah. It's grabbing at me."

"You need to ice it and then give it some heat."

Tiffany paused at her authoritativeness. She felt a pang of overstepping her boundaries. Baker didn't flinch. He was game.

"Oh yeah?" he said, teasingly. "You would know, Miss Basketball Star."

She eyed him playfully.

"I did my research on you," he said. "You were all-city your junior and senior seasons. One question though. With that resume, you should definitely be playing college ball. What's up?"

"I had offers."

"What happened?"

"Well, I felt like my body was breaking down. And I didn't have the drive to make it to the WNBA."

"Why not? If I were you and I had the opportunity to go pro, I'd at least give it a shot."

"Is that your motivation, Baker? To go to the NFL?"

"Me? No," he said, shaking his head. "This is my first season of actually being on the field. And I'm a senior. I'll be lucky if I get a D-Two scholarship offer. I just love the game. I want to keep playing for as long as I can. That's my motivation, I guess."

"You looked pretty special out there to me."

"I can't lie. It's a fantastic feeling, and me getting bigger and faster this past summer could definitely change things. Honestly, right now, being out there, balling out like that . . . "

Baker trailed off and Tiffany waited for him to finish his thought. He wasn't going to.

"Tell me about your body breaking down," he said.

"My legs," she said, nodding down to Baker's legs. "I did have hamstring issues, and they kept coming back. Always flaring up after games. I used that same treatment for three seasons, just to be able to play in games."

Baker watched Tiffany, falling deeper and deeper for her with each second they were together.

"I just got tired of it, you know?"

"Yeah. But how did you know when it was enough? When your body had had enough?"

"Easy. I tore my ACL in my last game. The Dallas City Championship. Didn't read that much about my career did you?"

Baker was silent.

"The game made my decision for me," she said. "After rehabbing for so long just to play, being able to walk normal again was an achievement. I made the decision to go to college and only be a student. That was enough for me."

"You didn't need the game anymore?"

"Nope. But realizing that took me some time."

Tiffany's wisdom was mind-blowing. The women—girls—he had spent time with up to that point were still locked in fazes of trivial insecurities situated around pockets of immaturity. He was searching for someone different, and here she was.

"What are you getting at with all of these questions?"

He thought about letting his guard down and alerting her to his concerns about the head injuries that he had sustained, as well as the potential ones in the future. But he did not let her in. Not because he wanted to hide anything from her or segregate her from his thoughts, he just didn't even know how he felt about this stuff yet. All he knew was that he wanted to keep playing for as long as fate would allow. Baker wasn't religious—something that would've been ridiculed mercilessly by Sandra—yet he also didn't want to test fate.

"Nothing," he said, finally. "Just thinking. Trying to get to know you better, that's all."

"You are a thinker, aren't you?"

"I guess."

Tiffany changed the subject after a prolonged

pause. "So, your mom is like a hot-shot professor, right?"

"I thought you've never taken one of her classes?"

"I haven't. But it's what I've heard. I'm planning to take her class on mixed-media in the spring."

"Yeah, I think she's well liked," Baker said. "My mom—she's awesome—she calmed me down after I got your number that day."

"Why did you need to be calmed down?"

"Are you kidding?" Baker asked with raised eyebrows. "I just got a fine college girl's number."

Tiffany would've blushed had she not averted her eyes from Baker's.

"And my worries aren't gone," Baker added. "I've been around college campuses my whole life. I know all the guys on campus aren't going to quit when they see you. How am I gonna sleep at night knowing that you're available?"

Tiffany turned her head and caught Baker's gaze head-on. "I'm not available."

Baker wasn't needy by any stretch, and he also had

a decent check on his ego, but it meant everything to hear Tiffany say that. She was beautiful, smart, and deep. There would be plenty of competition for her.

"Yeah?"

"Yeah."

Baker put his arms around Tiffany's waist. He leaned in for a kiss and brushed her cheek with his lips on the way in. Her body smelled fresh, yet her breath was a bit raw from the garlic and onions in the food. Baker didn't mind. He was starting to understand his mother's view of love and imperfection.

After a few kisses, Tiffany pulled away with a gasp. Baker looked down at the summer dress hugging her body. She had curves in all the right places. He looked down even further. Her open-toed sandals revealed feet that looked too pretty to be those of an athlete's.

"Easy, superstar," Tiffany said. "You're not gonna get it that easy."

"Huh?" Baker said, staggered and punch-drunk in love. "What do you mean?"

"You have to work."

"Work?"

She smiled an intoxicated smile. "Sure. You're not the type who's afraid of a little work, are you?"

Baker didn't want or expect Tiffany to be perfect, but he was beginning to think that she was perfect for him.

11

BAKER PLAYED LIKE A MAN POSSESSED DURING Churchill's next three games. His team dominated in each of the three wins, with its number-one receiver putting up a cumulative stat line of twenty-five catches for six hundred yards to go along with seven touchdowns. Baker also caught the eyes of a few local scouts during his tear. Forester fielded the calls in his office about this new receiver of his, this seemingly out-of-the-blue offensive threat. Forester told every inquiring mind the same thing: that Baker was a big-bodied receiver with soft hands and speed. He was an athlete, a worker, and a good person to boot.

For Baker, the most significant aspect of the past three games was that he did not take a single direct shot to the head. He was healthy—symptom-free—and happy going into Churchill's fifth game of the regular season. Baker was finally able to put the head injuries from early in the season in his past.

• •

"Hey hot-shot," Sandra said on the morning of Churchill's game against Taft High School. The crosstown rivalry had heated up in recent years when both programs lifted out of their respective funks. "Ready for the big game?"

"How do *you* know it's big game," Baker asked of his mother, with the dry wit usually reserved for Sandra's own use.

"I read the papers."

Baker laughed. "I'm ready. Yeah."

"Good. You look open in the eyes."

Sandra liked to use the term *open* when someone had focus and drive, a kind of quiet confidence in their craft.

"I feel open."

"Tiffany and I are going to sit next to each other during the game."

"Cool."

The bebop popped and flickered from Sandra's record player in the living room.

"I can see why you love football," Sandra said. "These last few weeks have taught me a lot about the game."

"Like what?"

"It's a thinking man's game," she said. "Before, I thought it was just a bunch of Neanderthals bashing each other's heads in. I see the strategy now."

Baker laughed again. His mother was really something.

"There is true thought and intention. I watch

you out there and *see* that you mean to use angles and things like that. I see you thinking."

"Well, yeah. Each play has a goal, and each player is taught a bunch of techniques to help their team achieve the goal."

"Duh," she said.

He had never broken it down in that fashion, but it was true. Football was more science than brute strength.

"I'm gonna head in early," he said, standing up from the kitchen table, empty plate in hand. "I wanna get a little treatment before first period."

Sandra stood up as well. Baker went to the sink to rinse his dish and then put it and the silverware he used into the dishwasher. He turned around to see Sandra standing right behind him.

"Whoa," he said.

"I just wanted to tell you how proud I am of you. Not because of your achievements, but because of your commitment. To your craft and your teammates. Believe me, I see a lot of lost young people on campus. The world would be a better place if it had more young people like you walking around."

Even though Baker and Sandra were the only two people in the kitchen, he felt uncomfortable with the praise. He did not want any kind of spotlight, nor was he playing for the praise or accolades. He just liked to work, and football was the current thing he was working on. Weeks before, he'd worried about losing football because of the blows to the head. He wasn't sure what his next endeavor would be. Now he simply wanted to continue riding this wave. Baker was open to the new and exciting possibilities afforded to him by the game.

"Thanks, Mom," he said. The last song of the album concluded in the other room, finishing with one last trumpet line. The only sounds now were pops and crackles of the vinyl as it continued spinning. Baker knew that sound from his childhood. He knew his mother needed the music, particularly early on, when his dad left and went out west. The old records gave Sandra something akin to what football's repetition and straightforwardness gave Baker.

The Taft game was important for early season playoff positioning. Four games in and it was clear to Forester that his team was dedicated, and explosive on offense. Aside from the poor defensive effort in game number one, that side of the ball was coming along as well. After being shredded on the ground against Clark, Churchill had given up an average of only seventy rushing yards in the last three contests. Though the defense wasn't quite at state championship level, its steady improvement, along with the prolific offense, put Churchill in the mix.

Baker was the unforeseen gift bestowed upon the squad. Forester knew what he would get from Ripley and Whitlock, for they were proven commodities. This wild card at receiver, however, seemed to have truly come from the beyond. Sure, the kid had speed. Every coach on staff could see that from day one of Baker's freshman season. A lot of kids had speed, but Baker had simultaneously unearthed the rare combination of speed, size, intellect, and heart that for so long had lain dormant inside him. Every season there were a few players that made slight jumps, but not many made the one that Baker had.

The team was loose about an hour before kickoff. The feeling in the locker room was one of quiet confidence borne out of preparation. Churchill's staff was one of the best in Texas at teaching situational football. Much of this came from Forester and his experience with improvisation in the Marines. He always told his players that the other team was motivated too, that Churchill could not always bank on out-hitting or overpowering the opponent. Sometimes, it was best to simply react, let the situation present itself, and approach a possible solution at full speed. Forester wanted his players playing with their hearts, bodies, and minds.

Baker was one of the loosest in the bunch. He

wasn't even supposed to be there in this position of prominence. He sat in front of his locker, playing out the Taft game in his mind. He visualized the opponent's defensive alignments, and then went through possible on-the-fly adjustments.

He enjoyed the mental part of it just as much as the physical. Ripley tapped Baker on the shoulder, knocking him out of his pregame trance.

"What's up, Bake?"

"Huh," Baker said, blinking lazily. "Just dreaming on it."

"You like all the crossing routes in the game plan?"

"We have to see if they go heavy with man coverage."

"They will. Their corners are tall. They don't have the hips for zone."

Ripley smiled because Baker was now a trusted friend and maybe even a bigger football nerd than Ripley himself.

"I want Coach to call some double-moves against them," Baker said.

"He will."

Forester sent the specialists out to warm up, and the rest of the players began finalizing their equipment decisions for the game.

"Have a good game," Ripley said, shaking Baker's hand and giving him a half-hug.

Taft had an early and surprising seven-to-nothing lead because of a kickoff return for a touchdown on the game's first play. Forester was disturbed by the special teams' gaffe, particularly because he had cut his teeth as a special teams' coach. He composed himself and addressed the starting offense directly before they hit the field. Forester wanted the unit to know that it had the serious responsibility of covering for another unit on the team. This communal approach to the brotherhood of the team helped each member forge a thick skin and cultivated a feeling of ownership and a deep fear of letting one another down, regardless of membership to the offense, defense, or special teams.

Baker took the early deficit in stride, as did Ripley, Whitlock, and the rest of the first-team offense. After jumping all over teams during the first month of the regular season, Churchill's offensive stars enjoyed this random, sudden drama. That drama was short lived, though, because on the first play of Churchill's drive, Ripley dropped back and hit Baker on one of the crossing routes that the team focused on during that week's practices. Baker outran first one of the gangly grasping-at-air cornerbacks, and then Taft's entire defense on the way to a touchdown.

The score was tied at seven after Baker's eighty-five-yard catch-and-run touchdown. After the play, Forester looked over at Hayes in disbelief. It wasn't that Baker had made the big play. The occurrences were becoming old hat for Baker. It was that the receiver was actually getting better each week.

Churchill's capacity crowd was at full throat.

Ripley grabbed Baker by the shoulder pads on the sidelines.

"Baker!" he screamed. "Baker!"

This simple utterance was all Ripley needed to express himself. It was all anyone around Churchill's sidelines needed to understand the moment. The people at the game were witness to something remarkable. Witness to what hard work and dedication could get you. In Baker's case, somehow, his true potential had been hidden for years, perhaps just below the surface.

After the ensuing kickoff, Taft began its drive at their own twenty-two yard line. Churchill's defense was as eager as the offense to show its stuff, forcing Taft to go three and out before punting.

The scene at the stadium was now one step below frenzy, with the next big play by Churchill ready to push it over the edge. Baker hoped to provide the big play, for despite being a good sportsman, he was also all about pushing the opponent to the point of submission.

On the first play of Churchill's second offensive possession, Baker threw a jarring, crack-down block on one of Taft's unsuspecting defensive ends. The block not only sprung Whitlock for a long gain, but it also rattled the defender's bones. Baker helped the opposing player off the turf and patted him on the helmet. The beleaguered defensive end still didn't know what hit him by the time he stumbled over to the Taft's sideline for refuge. Baker didn't mean to be harsh with the crushing block, but intimidation was a very real part of football. Those who thought otherwise were fooling themselves.

Ripley dropped back on the following play and looped a fade into the right corner of the end zone. Baker, with one of Taft's long corners draped over him, leapt into the air and snagged the ball with a grace that was more ballerina than football player. He had officially taken the game over. After the extra point, Churchill was ahead by fourteen to seven.

The route began during Taft's next drive. Churchill's defense forced a fumble and ran it back for a touchdown. The Churchill run defense had given up two yards on the ground—a far cry from its opening effort against Clark. The score was twenty-one to seven after the extra point.

Forester stalked up and down the sideline with his heart beating in and out of his chest. This was not usually his style, but he sensed that something big was happening with his team. He wanted his players to know that they had an opportunity in front of them. And to become that team, his players would have to push Taft off the ledge.

"One more!" Forester yelled to his charges. "Score one more time and they'll cave!"

For good measure, Churchill did tack on another touchdown before halftime—a fifty yard off-tackle run by Whitlock. Churchill's players ran into the locker room leading Taft twenty-eight to seven, knowing that this was, in fact, their time.

· ·

Forester reiterated the need to crush Taft's spirit during the intermission. Blood was in the water for Churchill's fans as well. They could sense that Taft was ready for the slaughter, with no need to delay the inevitable. Despite popular belief, football is not an intentionally cruel sport. In fact, it is incumbent on the better team to dispatch the lesser one with as little pain as possible.

Churchill's offense took the field after a touchback to open the third quarter. Baker beat press coverage and unleashed a double-move on Taft's strong safety. Ripley let the pass fly and just barely overthrew Baker. The missed opportunity was not a total exercise in futility, however; the aggressive play call set a precedent for how Churchill would approach not only the rest of the game but also the balance of the season. Churchill would continue to throw the ball downfield, and play to win.

Ripley handed the ball off to Whitlock on the next play, and he carried it for five yards. The next play call on third and five was meant to attack Taft's tall but stiff cornerbacks. Churchill's crossing route combinations had been giving Taft's defense trouble all game. Baker loved the aggressive play call, even with the healthy lead. It didn't hurt that Ripley would look his way first and allow him the opportunity to put more of his fingerprints on the game.

One of the seven deadly sins that football fed into, however, was greed, and even Baker was not immune. With each passing week, his confidence had grown, and with that growth came the inescapable lust for more: more responsibility, more production. True, it was a hunger for more stats, but there was something more primal at work as well. It was the need to kill the wounded antelope.

Baker was one of many in Churchill's pride that felt the need to deal Taft its fatal blow.

At the snap, Baker shot off the line of scrimmage at a straight angle. He created instant separation from the overmatched cornerback who tried in vain to bend his knees and give chase. The space between Baker and the corner was widening with each passing millisecond. This time—and for the first time all game—Taft's middle linebacker recognized Churchill's plan of attack.

The linebacker sat down in the middle of the field, and waited. He waited for Baker to come his way on the shallow cross. When Ripley saw the space that Baker had created, he lapsed, forgetting that there was the possibility of danger in the center of Taft's defense. The middle linebacker was that danger.

Ripley's pass led Baker a hair too much. The middle linebacker timed his attack, recoiling like a cobra, striking at the very moment when Baker and the ball met. For Baker, the crown of the middle linebacker's helmet caught him right underneath the chin.

There was a sickening clack of plastic on plastic that reverberated around the stadium. Sandra and Tiffany cringed in the stands. It wasn't until the dust settled that they realized that it was Baker lying motionless on the field. Though the hit itself was brutal, the inherent danger in it was unprejudiced. Taft's middle linebacker sprung to his feet unscathed and motioned to both sidelines that there was something wrong with the receiver he had just clobbered. The middle linebacker had no wish to "send a message" to Baker and the entire grandstanding Churchill offense. The hit was a simple football play and, in all actuality, a hell of a read by the middle linebacker.

Sandra and Tiffany exited their row in the stands and looked for the fastest entry onto the field. The middle linebacker dropped to one knee and bowed his head as the medical staff from both teams, along with Forester and Hayes, descended on an unconscious, and shallow breathing Baker.

12

IT WAS NEITHER FATE NOR DESTINY THAT BROUGHT Baker to this place. The game did not work in that way; the actions, the techniques, the intentions, were all up to chance. There were plays that mimicked the carnage of car wrecks, while others were benign, giving off an appearance of ease. The problem is, the human brain is not meant to react in such a violent way that quickly. A buzzing bee around the face causes a reaction, a fear reaction that takes time—time that the brain needs to tell your hand to swat the bee away. Football is similar to life in many ways but also very different. The probability of falling down during each play and then having to get right back up affords the individual the opportunity to experience life's ebbs and flows on a symbolic level. The differences, however, can mean life and death.

In football, time is a commodity that is always fleeting; the game clock is running, and the play clock is close behind. Each snap is a gasping, fly-by-the-seat-of-your-pants rollercoaster that at its very best is a fierce test of wills, and at its worst, a clustered, incomprehensible mess. A player never has enough time to react. Players have been taught to smack the hell out of a wide receiver who buzzes across their face. "Hit anything that moves," goes the mantra. A quarterback drops back and doesn't see the blitzing defender from the blind-side. In civilized society that's called assault. On the football field, that's called "barbecue chicken."

No, it's not about fate or destiny. Those words are too divine for the football field. Football is a strict game of chance where the practitioners are constantly, maybe even stupidly, risking it all. The game's beauty derives from that need of risk that's set deep down inside us all—the same need that informs the choice of one putting their hand next to that flame. It's primordial.

For Baker, the moment of risking it all had arrived.

* * *

The hit rattled Baker so completely that he lay unconscious in a nearby hospital hours after the remainder of the Taft game was cancelled. There were tubes doing his breathing for him, and Sandra—the only person allowed in the room—watched her son, squeezing his hand at random intervals. His father was on the way from California, but the doctors made no guarantees. Tiffany stood alone in the waiting room. Forester, Hayes, and Nathan, along with Ripley and Whitlock and a few other teammates tried to bypass hospital protocol but could not gain entrance to Baker's room.

Baker had faint brain activity but there were no

signs beyond that. If it were not for the tubes, the oxygen to his brain would be cut off. The hope now was that he would come out of the coma so that his organs could begin running on their own again. The doctors didn't know much.

Sandra decided that she was not going to cry—that even though he was unconscious, her tears would affect him. The range of emotions swirling through her were enough to kill her. She didn't know if she'd make it through the night.

A nurse entered and put a hand on Sandra's shoulder. "Why don't you go into the waiting room and close your eyes for a little bit? I'll come get you if anything changes."

"I . . . " Sandra said, quietly. "I don't want to leave. I mean, I don't want to be away if he . . . "

"Just go close your eyes for a little while. I promise, I'll come get you if he wakes up."

The nurse took Sandra's hand and squeezed it.

Sandra walked to the door of Baker's hospital room. She turned around to look back at her son.

Tubes aside, he was relaxed. His strong, sure hands were loose by his sides. His mouth was curled into a smile around the breathing tube.

The waiting room was breathless as Sandra entered. She walked right over to Tiffany and sat down in the empty chair next to her.

"Anything?" Tiffany whispered.

Sandra shook her head. Tiffany began to sob and it made no sound. Sandra put her arm around Tiffany, but she was not going to cry.

Forester and the rest of Churchill's contingent neared the two women. Forester sat down next to Sandra. She turned to face him, and her countenance was expressionless. He put his arm around her and squeezed tight and began to cry. The situation reminded him of his time in Iraq, when members of his unit were wounded in battle.

Once Coach began to cry, nearly everyone in the waiting room was shedding tears—everyone but Sandra. She was not religious, spiritual, or even the least bit superstitious. But at that moment, she believed that her son would die if she cried.

13

BAKER WAS ON A FIELD. HE DIDN'T KNOW EXACTLY which field it was but it was definitely one from his childhood. This place where he stood was not scary; it was just empty. The weeds were golden, baked in the sun for far too long. The surrounding tree line was dry and harsh. The trees were in desperate need of water.

There wasn't much Baker could do with no one else around. He had waited his entire life; what harm would a little more waiting do?

Something changed in an instant. The light changed around the field. The high, persistent sun started its descent. Suddenly, the outer edges of the field were in darkness. Baker was glued to his spot now. There was an evil—bringing a stinging miasma with it—at the edges of the field. He could not see the evil but could smell it. He knew it was there.

* * *

It was Baker's third day at the hospital, and there was still no change. Sandra sat by his bed, and alongside her was Baker's father, Harold, who had come to Texas earlier than expected and under different circumstance. There were no updates from the doctors because according to them, the brain was still the great unknown. All they could do was wait.

"Want me to go get you some coffee?" Harold asked.

"I'm fine."

"You should eat something or go for walk," he persisted. "I'll stay here with James."

Sandra glared at her ex-husband. She tried with

all her might not to take anything out on him. After all, this wasn't his fault. Her glare softened and she stood up with a heavy sigh.

"Okay," she said. "I'm gonna go home and take a shower and change."

Harold nodded and Sandra left the room. He moved closer to his son and bent down to get a good look at his face behind the breathing tube. Baker seemed to be resting comfortably. Though Harold was gone a lot of the time, he knew his son.

All things considered, he and Baker had a good relationship. After the divorce and Harold's move out west, their relationship was mainly forged through trips during Baker's Christmas and summer breaks. Harold flashed on a few of the bonding memories and smiled, before the immediacy of the moment just below his line of vision washed it all away with the harshest possible rush.

With football taking precedence, Baker's last summer was spent toiling out in the San Antonio sun instead of exploring the European countryside with

Harold. The disappointment of a summer without his son was hard at first, but Harold doubled-down on the phone calls and planned to attend at least one game that season. By chance, he had planned to show up to Churchill's game the following week.

After the nurse came to check Baker's vitals, Harold moved a chair close to his son and sat. He took Baker's hand in his own.

"I'm here, son," Harold said. "I love you and I'm here."

"I'm here, son."

The sound came at Baker as if he were in an echo chamber. Or as if he were underwater.

"I love you and I'm here."

He couldn't place the voice. Nothing was comprehensible in this place, though at the same time, any and everything seemed possible. Baker could hear shallow breathing now. And he felt stronger, like there was a brewing vitality all around. The field's grass was cut and manicured and verdant now. Gone was the murk of uncertainty. The sun was back and high in its usual perch. There were even more voices now, all around him. Baker began running on the fresh, green grass. He was gaining momentum. There was nothing in his way, no impediment until the field came to an end and Baker reached the edge. It was a cliff that opened into an abyss.

"I'm here, son."

Baker looked down and realized nothing.

"I love you and I'm here."

• •

Harold and Sandra took turns with Baker at the hospital. It's not that they couldn't stand to be around one another, it was more to avoid the burnout that comes from staying by a hospital bed for hours on end. Also, there was no update on Baker's condition. His coma was a week old, and there was simply no way to tell. Forester came by the hospital every day after school. Churchill's game was cancelled that week.

Forester felt a pang of guilt each time he saw an unconscious Baker lying there in bed, unable to chase his dream. The guilt was crushing although Forester did not exactly blame himself. His was more of the inevitable, and probably unavoidable, kind of guilt.

Sandra held herself together admirably, keeping her no-cry pact in stone. Tiffany stopped by a lot as well, in between her week of classes. Once Baker was stabilized, the hospital relaxed its policy and allowed for friends and teammates to spend some time in his room. Tiffany sat up with Baker—just the two of them—talking to him, squeezing his hand, for four nights in a row. She loved him even though she hadn't been given the opportunity to know him all that well.

During the first night, she was angry, feeling robbed that the person she found in this world to love may be taken away. The second night was drenched in extreme and violent sadness—a tear-filled and puffy-eyed night. The third night was much like the second. On the fourth night, Tiffany reverted back to anger.

One night, late, Harold found Forester standing next to the vending machines in an adjoining corridor on Baker's floor. Forester's eyes were heavy and brooding. He looked like a man who didn't want to go home and face sleep. The morning could not come fast enough.

"Harold," Forester said in a gruff voice.

"Hi, Coach Forester."

"Please. Call me, Monty."

"Okay, Monty."

"How's he doing?"

"Same. The doctors don't know if he'll pull through. They don't seem to know much actually."

"If anybody can pull through, it's your son."

"Thank you, Monty."

"I mean it."

"I'm sure you do. But the fact of the matter is

that no one—*no one*—knows for sure how brain injuries will react."

Forester thought about the offseason coaching clinics, the lectures on how to teach better form-tackling in practices. He knew these things were good for the game, especially over time, but there was no way to legislate the immediate, present-day danger out of the game. Any positive changes would be felt gradually and incrementally.

"I know James is a strong kid," Harold said, "but I just don't know if that matters."

"You're probably right," Forester said, defeated.

"There's risk involved in the game," Harold said. "Everyone who plays knows it. Or they should know it."

"They know it," Forester said.

Harold could see something in Forester's eyes—something that needed to be hashed out, pored over. Harold could not help him do so, however. He had to worry about his son in the ICU.

"Well, I'm going to get back," Harold said. "Good night."

"Okay."

Harold turned to leave but turned back to Forester first.

"Go home and sleep. There's nothing you can do here. Just hope, or pray, if it suits you."

Harold walked back down the corridor and turned the corner toward Baker's room. Forester stayed where he was until he was able to get in and see Baker in the morning.

* * *

There's not much time left in the game, Baker thought, with a new setting placed before him, a new horizon to lock his gaze upon. *I just have this feeling.*

The game was over. Baker had played valiantly and battled to the end. There was no clear winner anointed or loser ridiculed. It just ended. Baker looked out at the cool, cerulean ocean. There was a pleasant breeze at his back, and he made sure to take note of it. He looked up and out, following the infinite horizon. There was a swirling out there, a gathering storm. His chest heaved and it wobbled the wide panorama.

What's happening? he thought. Wait a minute.

Baker wasn't scared of this new unknown; he just wanted to settle into his new existence. Someone pressed their hand against his forehead. It was cool and probably possessed a death-like grip. Baker looked and saw a spotlight overhead. It was piercing and sharp, instigating, in a way. The hand kneaded him. He could probably fathom what was to come.

On the following Saturday, exactly eight days after Baker took the hit in the middle of the field and slipped into the coma, the neurologist was in Baker's room with Sandra, Harold, and Tiffany. The doctor, an older white man with silver hair and blue eyes, stood over Baker. His flashlight was on and its beam was poised onto Baker's peeled-back eyes. The doctor then touched Baker's face and noted its warmth. The production of sweat on his patient's forehead represented a new hope that Baker would pull through.

"We think he squeezed my hand last night," Sandra said from behind.

"That's a possibility," the doctor said over his shoulder. "The sweat production gives me hope."

He turned around and faced the expectant family.

"Something is happening with James," he said. "There's clearly brain activity happening and some biological functions too."

"Is it a sign?" Sandra asked.

"It could be."

The family didn't want to say another word because more questions might've brought on a less optimistic forecast. The doctor covered himself anyway.

"But it may mean nothing," he said. "These next

few hours are important if James is going to wake up."

The doctor left Baker's room and his family watched him fight from a distance. Sandra approached first, then Harold, and finally, Tiffany.

"I love you, son," Sandra said.

"Keep fighting, my boy," Harold said.

When Tiffany cried, Baker's parents didn't mind. They wanted to cry as well now; but between Sandra's pact and Harold's naturally stoic nature, there was no way.

"We love you, Baker," Tiffany said.

14

James Baker was not in a fighting mood. He was tired. And this business of trading places, one background for the next, was the most tiresome of all. Baker was beyond understanding. He was free to go with the wind, or the river. *Now if there were only a river to follow*, he thought.

The overhead lights were gone. There was no cold hand on his head either. "It didn't have to be this way," his mother Sandra would probably say.

"Well, how would you have it happen then?" Baker would most likely reply.

He was not in a fighting mood anymore. No

debates. No politics. He was in the mood to rest. But it could've gone either way. Baker focused on the things around him. He closed his eyes tight and wondered if he could decide his own fate, or write his own story. Baker put everything he had into it. He believed in the power of the mind, as taught to him by his mother and father.

Baker had enough time to write one more chapter. He held the pen. It was time. Finally. He centered himself in the middle of the field. The game was tight, one of those nail-biters that people remember for years, with less than one minute left on the clock. But there was a lot left that was unfamiliar to Baker. The stadium was not Churchill's, or any other that he had played in for that matter. Baker didn't recognize any of his teammates or opponents either. They had no faces. The coaches were in the dark. The sidelines, shrouded in mist—a noir-inspired shadowland. It was raining now, that steady, unnerving patter from above. Baker looked up through his facemask and all he saw was gray. *There's time for one more play,* he thought.

In the huddle, Baker received no play call, no route, no instructions on how to get his job done.

All he heard was:

"I love you, son."

"Keep fighting, my boy."

"We love you, Baker."

He heard each of those things once and then the huddle was broken. Baker approached the line of scrimmage on the right side of the formation, his usual spot. The strong side.

That phantom of a quarterback called out the play, some indecipherable mix of symbols and tongues that Baker could not have dreamed of understanding. All Baker knew was to go full speed. He'd do that one more time because that was all there was time for.

The ball was snapped.

Baker shot off the line. One by one, a defense filled with goblins disappeared from his path. His offensive teammates disappeared into thin air next, until it was just Baker and the quarterback on the field. He looked back as he continued running his route. The ball was released, and then the quarterback was gone. Baker saw the ball in the air, tracked it, and waited. He ran as the ball neared him. When he gathered his focus in preparation to make the catch, Baker looked up and lost the ball. He heard no crowd noise, no reaction to the unsuccessful play. Baker continued running.

He woke, somewhere, lying on his back. He gazed up at an overhead light—a bright, white one. The room was white all around too, but it was an unnatural white, a white of fluorescence. The light pulsed but did not gain on Baker. Nor did he get closer to it. It stayed in its place above him. The thing under his back felt metallic and somehow sterile.

Baker was outside of himself, watching this version of himself.

He blinked a couple of times and the blurry, white image—most likely a ceiling—stared back at him.

"Is it worth it?" he mumbled.

It wasn't the first time the thought ever crossed his mind, but it was the first time he'd ever spoken the words out loud. The problem was, without football, he didn't know who he was. Or what he would become. The thought scared him. He could hear the crowd now, roaring over top. His hearing was fine, but his vision was not. It sounded like the crowd was angry at the referee about a call, or perhaps his team scored another touchdown. He wasn't sure.

He sat up slowly, and his whole body felt like it was stuck in gelatin. He was truly frozen. The door opened and someone walked in. He couldn't see their face because of the blurred vision.

"James," he said.

"Yeah?" Baker replied.

"How's the head?"

"Who? Who are you?"

"I'm Don—the head trainer of the varsity football team. The Mustangs."

"Oh."

"You took a pretty good shot. Your bell got rung, but you'll be okay in the morning."

"I don't feel okay. Besides, don't I play for Churchill High School? I'm a Churchill Charger. I'm no Mustang. And your name is Don? The trainer at my school goes by the name of Nathan."

"Bell just got rung, is all."

Don stood in front of Baker and tilted up his chin so that they were eye to eye. Baker could see the whites of Don's eyes rolling around in their sockets, examining him.

"Lie back down," Don said, as the crowd roared again. The sound of it was nearing.

"If you get nauseous, holler," Don concluded.

He helped Baker to lie back down. As soon as Baker's eyes blinked on the white ceiling, he asked himself again, "Is it worth it?"

Don turned off the overhead light before exiting the room. The room was cool, dark, and dry now.

Baker waited for one final indication from the crowd. He wanted to know how the game turned out.